MW01126735

A. ERIN WALKER

Away

The Search for Oneself May Result in the
Danger of Alternative Discoveries...

A Novel by A. Erin Walker

For my support team, thank you.
As well as anyone in need of a little inspiration to live the best life they can. Let's never settle for anything less.

a·way

/əˈwā/

adverb
adverb: away

1. To or at a distance from a particular place, person, or thing.
2. Toward or into nonexistence
3. Constantly, persistently or continuously

Prologue.

The dream was recurring.

There is a glass box the size of an auditorium with no doors or windows. I am inside in the midst of what appears to be a party with all attendees adorned in outfits of gray from head to toe.

Gray heels. Gray ties. Gray jeans. Gray eyes.

There is a band playing loud, obnoxious swing music that everyone is dancing or bobbing their heads to as they indulge in their hors d'oeuvres. There is also laughter, lust, and joy.

And then there is me.

I have been standing in the corner, alone, inspecting the glass dome that covers us all. Staring out into the mysterious world of bright, white lights I can only assume those are what we are supposed to be protected from. But I want nothing more than to be released from this safety.

Why are there no doors? Why am I even in here?

Beads of sweat begin to form on my forehead as my curiosity transforms into obsession. I begin to push on the glass to see if it will slide open but to no avail. I back up and stomp my heels as I spring forward to ram my body into it with the hopes that the glass will shatter all over the linoleum flooring.

Fail.

I can feel myself losing control of my emotions as fear and anxiety take over in my unsuccessful attempts to escape the enclosure. The frustration manifests as I pick up the closest items I can find; platters of finger sandwiches, centerpieces from the gray-covered tables, chairs, etc. I throw them at the glass just to watch them bounce off and hit the floor without even a scratch.

It's taunting me.

The music gets louder and my heart beats faster as I search the party for anyone sharing in my desperation, but they are mostly oblivious while those who have taken notice scoff at my attacks toward my inanimate enemy. Am I the only one that sees the possibility that this "protector" may really be the opponent?

I can't breathe.

AWAY

The more I continue to fail at my escape, the less air I seem to have. I start to hyperventilate and the people around me immerse themselves in the party, having the time of their lives as if my suffering and I do not exist. How are we in such close vicinity yet they pretend as though I am in another world?

Maybe I am? What the hell?

I make my way back to the corner and crawl up against the glass, accepting defeat as I lose more and more of my ability to inhale. Rocking my body back and forth to distract me from the feeling of my lungs being squeezed to bits, I close my eyes as the final draws of air leave my body until I am left with nothing.

One.

Cleveland-Hopkins International Airport, Present Day

I knew that if I didn't do it now, it would never happen.

I have chosen a window seat that is located a couple of rows behind the wings of the plane, just how my mom always taught me to. My fingers trace across my name printed on the boarding pass, "BRYANT, TAMRYN" and I patiently await takeoff, but my mind is going non-stop.

For a long time now, I have been unable to resonate with this life. Besides my loving parents and a few friends I have made, the environment of my hometown always felt more foreign than homey.

Three years ago I graduated from high school and went to a small, public college about an hour away from where I grew up in Cleveland, Ohio. Prior to this, my high school career was busy with volleyball, participation in student council, volunteer work on the weekends, and the occasional house party with friends. All of this while maintaining a 3.9 GPA that was disappointing because I failed to reach 4.0.

Ultimately, I knew that I did well and choosing to further my education like everyone else brought a sense of accomplishment and made my parents proud.

The number one thing I had always wanted was for my mother and father to be happy for me. I was always the "good girl" in school and tried my best to excel in every endeavor, simply because they always supported my decisions and I would have hated to let them down.

I had no initial plans of what I wanted to major in, so I chose Business Administration because it seemed safe; something that could help me earn a substantial income. Even though I wasn't entirely sure of what I saw myself doing for the rest of my life, the fact that I was accepted into college was all I needed to feel successful.

Most of my peers were in the same boat.

Those who were ahead of me encouraged the rest of us, "You've got time to figure everything out. It will all come together, eventually."

But then the dream started to appear.

The first time it ever decided to invade my slumber was sometime during the first week of my college career. I startled awake in the long, twin-sized bed provided by the university, hot and gasping for air. Sweat dripped from the tip of my nose and I placed my hand over the rapidly beating heart inside of my chest.

I forced my thoughts into a stream of positivity to calm my nerves, "*You are in a new place, Tam. The change is just picking with you. You'll get used to it. Nightmares are normal.*"

My dorm room was the size of a janitor's closet.

The nighttime darkness that filled it did not immediately sit well with my vision, and my body did not hesitate to inform me that I had to pee.

So, I reached for the lamp that rested on the nightstand and light then filled the space, revealing my roommate lying in her bed looking at me with wrinkles of worry across her forehead, "What in the motherfuck, Tamryn... Are you okay?"

The dream did not occur for the rest of the school year, and I finished my first year of college with a cumulative GPA of 3.7, making the Dean's list.

One afternoon when I was back in my hometown for summer vacation, I hung out with a friend of mine named Dana, who decided she wasn't returning to school in the fall.

"I just don't see the point."

A look of bewilderment glowed through my eyes. "How could you not see the point in gaining a college education?" I said.

We were sitting on her porch and her three little sisters were dancing and playing in the sprinklers set up in the front yard. The sun was bright, shining down on the city with its powerful radiation and I silently scolded myself for wearing jeans that day.

"College is building up a hell of a lot of debt, and I'm struggling extra hard to afford it and remain focused for what?" Dana keeps an eye on her siblings as she speaks. "For me to spend the rest of my life working a dead-end job in order to pay off that debt? And hoping I have just enough left over to help out my family along the way and *maybe* get a house one day? I might as well start getting paid now and not have to worry about all of that. I don't see the point."

College does come with a boatload of hard work for many hopes and possibilities and few guarantees, but it's what we are expected to do.

It is what we are *supposed* to do.

You get your high school diploma, get your Bachelor's degree, get your Master's if you wish to earn an above average wage, and get your doctorate if you want everyone to know you are the shit. The idea is you get the most education you can to gain access to the most opportunities of those hopes and possibilities. That's just how life goes.

Right?

My talk with Dana is what brought the doubts hiding deep down in the abyss of my subconscious to the surface. I was becoming more and more concerned of the path I had chosen as I realized that it is not necessarily a path that *Tamryn* chose. I let the world choose it for me and now I was curious about what other options were out there. Options that were more along the lines of putting effort into figuring out what I want before eventually. Why should I endure an experience that promises to deliver a life of substance, yet is equipped with an illegible disclaimer at the bottom of the screen warning of the obstacles that most people tend to face post-degree?

I just don't want to waste my life.

And this is why I went from believing that college was the best choice for me to only following through because I had already started. This change in my mindset triggered a huge change in my actions, and like a bullet fired from a gun there was no coming back from it.

I continued to go through the motions during my sophomore year, but nothing was the same. The more I thought and questioned, the more out of place I felt. It was as if I was wasting more and more of my life away with stress-filled days, trying to do well on exams rather than actually learning.

This path may work for some, but was not working for me.

Hearing how "everyone else is going through it too" was not enough to make it okay anymore.

And there was still that damn dream.

It started to recur so often that I learned to expect it at least once or twice a week. I would analyze it in the morning during my walk to classes, and I was eventually forced to conclude that a higher power was trying to communicate a truth that I did not want to accept.

I was extremely unhappy.

My overall focus on school was thrown. First, the parties became more desirable than the late-night study sessions. Then, the sex buddies became more interesting than getting to class on time or even at all. And finally, an emptiness formed inside of me that neither of the former could fill.

There was no Dean's list at the end of sophomore year and a major drop in my GPA, along with very little desire to return when the summer ended. My parents voiced their concern with hints of disappointment, which added fuel to a fire they may not have intended to feed. How can I make them proud if I am not even proud of myself?

I began to communicate more with my friends and associates that either dropped out or never even gave college a chance after high school. I stayed in constant contact with Dana, who was now working a factory job, driving a new car, and pregnant. I also stayed in touch with friends of friends who built their own brands, and those who are happily making tons of money moving up in career fields that do not require degrees. But, then there are some who dropped out and moved to their dream city, just to end up right back where they started.

It may not always bring a happy ending, but none of these people let the world choose their path.

They made their own way and either became self-made or got pushed back to start. There was no luck required, just a strong dedication to a passion. And even if they were forced to start over due to a bump in the road, they still worked hard at constructing a new route.

I want to be that type of person.

My passion is to be willing to leave the safety of normalcy.

A majority of the people I have observed around me find solace in being right next to every one else. Just like they were blind to my desperation to break free in my dream, they appear oblivious to the distance they can go with a change in perspective. And why must the few who dare to dream bigger than the rest be faced with the threat of being dragged into misery rather than receiving encouragement? They want to see you doing well but if you ever start to do better than them, they'll tear down your goals for the temporary gratification that they made the right decision in being basic.

I trace my fingers across the destination of my boarding pass marked in black lettering, "LAX", and recalled the moment I informed my parents of the new direction I mapped out for myself.

Fall semester of my junior year released into winter break, returning me back home and I knew, no matter what my mom and dad had to say, that I would not be making that hour drive back to campus for spring semester. I'm moving to Los Angeles, California and staying with my cousin Melanie who has been living there for about eight years now, since she graduated from high school and turned eighteen. I have never been to California, but Melanie is like a sister to me and anywhere that she is, I know I will be okay.

It was the day after Christmas and the day before my twenty-first birthday:

"I am young and I am learning. I have made mistakes and I know that I will make plenty more. This may be a mistake in itself, but sometimes bad decisions land you in the right places. I just want to give myself a chance to end up in the right place, rather than end up in the wrong place forever due to contentment or fear. Instead of going back to school in a couple weeks, I want to move to LA with Melanie. She's been making sure that I am serious and promises she will look out for me. I still have all the money in my savings and she said I can stay with her as long as I need to… The worst that could happen is I end up back here and in school where I

started. I just have to know for sure that I am not wasting my life away."

I could tell it was not something my parents were expecting to hear and a change they were reluctant to back. Yet, since they were never the type of parents to dictate my life and the strength of their love for me shows in their willingness to allow me to make my own decisions, the constant support continued.

They purchased the one-way ticket to my destination, emailing the itinerary to me in less than twenty-four hours in time for it to be the best birthday gift I could ask for.

So, here I am. Awaiting the takeoff of a brand new chapter in my life, with big hopes to discover who I am on my own terms and evade the glass dome of my nightmares before it is too late.

Two.

Los Angeles, Present Day

Sunshine. Palm Trees. Oh, the humidity.

I take a breath of fresh air and scratch through my thick, curly hair as I step out into the terminal from baggage claim. I am excited to be where I am, but even more excited to see Melanie. As mentioned before, she moved eight years ago right after receiving her high school diploma and the summer before my freshman year. She had always been like an older sister to me and we have always stayed close despite the distance. She has not been back to Ohio since she moved, so I have only seen her on video messaging platforms and social networks ever since.

◇

AWAY

In order to fully understand Melanie, one must understand her upbringing.

She was raised by our Aunt Shannon, and while they were cordial they were not that close.

Shannon had endured a great deal of heartbreak in her life, having lost her husband, our Uncle Mark, to a fatal car crash and just a few years after losing him, she grew close to a man named Travis whom she dated for a while before their relationship ended abruptly. She stayed close to family after the death of Mark and tried to remain positive while being faced with the pressure to take care of Melanie on her own. Yet, when things went south with Travis, it took a while for her to even inform anybody of the relationship ending.

Through all of this, Shannon never seemed to be cruel to Melanie, just unaffectionate and distant. But, Melanie always appeared to be unfazed by it.

It is almost as if Melanie was prepared for this outcome, already being denied any relationship with her parents; her mother making it clear when she was a baby that she did not want her and her father never being around to begin with. So how much damage could one more strained kinship cause?

Melanie's mom, Lucille, is the middle child under Shannon and older than my mother, Patricia. She was always the daughter who gave my grandparents the most problems growing up and nothing changed when the three sisters became grown women.

Lucille was sandwiched between an all-star older sister whose straight A's and athletic ability in basketball got her a full-ride in college and a little sister that always got whatever she wanted for being mommy and daddy's *baby girl*. Before Patricia was born, Lucille may have been the baby of the family but she was faced with the challenge of living in Shannon's shadow. Shannon had been bringing in trophies and honor roll certificates since elementary school, while Lucille had yet to find her niche and seemed to have misplaced her inherited intelligence.

After Patricia arrived, Lucille witnessed her new little sister receive showers of love and affection that she never seemed to experience when she was the youngest. I am sure my grandparents never meant to display favoritism amongst their daughters, but Lucille felt so overlooked her whole life and started to find the worst ways to receive the attention that she craved.

As the sisters grew older, Lucille allowed herself to get tied up with the wrong crowd and would be caught engaging in activities a young girl should not be caught doing (especially under the stairwells inside of her high school). This forced her mother and father to tend to her cries for attention, but her wrongdoings only attracted negative responses from them instead of sympathy and affection that she longed for.

When she could not shake the feeling that she would never be loved as much as her siblings, her cries for attention became cries for help as she continued the rebellious behavior to help her cope with how she felt.

Staying out late turned into being brought home by police officers which escalated to her experimenting with drugs. Lucille was put on lock down, a punishment so aggressive that kept her under constant surveillance by her parents and required her teachers to contact them if Lucille did so much as forget to raise her hand before she spoke. Once she graduated from high school and turned eighteen, she moved out to escape my grandparents and all of the real trouble had begun.

The family would only hear from her occasionally over a span of many years, short phone calls saying she was still alive and updates on which friends she was living with at the moment.

Shannon had received her nursing degree and gotten engaged to Mark Williams while Patricia was still in the midst of her own college career. Everyone continued to move on with their lives, putting no extreme effort into ending the seclusion Lucille had placed herself into.

She had always been the black sheep of the family that liked to go her own way, and no matter what small offers were made for her to come home she would always refuse and insist that her distance was best for everyone. She was supposed to be in Shannon's wedding but would always end up missing in action when it was time for meetings or dress fittings, unsurprisingly skipping the entire wedding ceremony altogether. This put a crack in her relationship with Shannon and raised alarm throughout the family similar to the foresight of a natural disaster. Everyone knew Lucille to be a seeker of attention but would never imagine that she would take it that far.

A collect call from a pay phone interrupted the newlywed's sleep a few weeks later. Powered by the sounds of sobs and apologies that seeped through the phone line from Lucille's slurred voice and transformed themselves into tears spilling down Shannon's face.

Something was very wrong with her little sister and regardless of everything she had done, she knew action needed to be taken. Shannon was still her big sister and felt the need to do whatever she could in order to make sure she was okay, as long as Lucille allowed her to.

So she asked where Lucille was and got in the car with her husband, prepared to bring her sister home for good.

The address Shannon was given had the navigation system lead them into the slums of the city and they found her amongst a group of drug addicts on a street lined with abandoned houses.

She fit in so well with her worn, decrepit clothing and drastic weight loss that Shannon almost didn't recognize her.

They replaced the plan of taking her home with taking her straight to a hospital which led to her checking into a rehabilitation center. After about six months of the most intense program the center could offer, Lucille had become clean of her heroine addiction and displayed the sincerest gratitude to her sister for being there to save her in the darkest hour of her life.

She was released from the center, moved in with Shannon and Mark, and continued to progress from there.

About two years came and went and Lucille had been working a steady job as well as dating someone on a supposedly serious level. She never wanted to bring the guy around Shannon or the rest of the family, which they assumed to just be her usual secretive preference. Their greatest and only real concern was that she was clean and happy, so they didn't pressure her into introducing the mystery man.

However, once it was discovered that Lucille was pregnant, they expected to be meeting the father of the baby sooner or later.

As told by Lucille, he was just as excited about the pregnancy as she was and there were plans made for them to live together and get married upon the arrival of their baby. Time seemed to fly by and before anyone saw it coming, the due date was right around the corner. The house was crowded with presents wrapped in pink that came flowing in when Lucille had announced that she was expecting a baby girl. Everyone was waiting to receive that "It's time!" call for the little princess to make her grand entrance into the world.

Then the baby's father started to act up.

The man that Lucille referred to as her "personal gift from God" and the "love of her life" wasn't calling as much to check on her. She could rarely get him to show up to take her to his house as he used to do almost everyday, and whenever they did speak he always found something to fight with her about. Lucille felt as though the pressure of becoming a father in a few days was starting to get to his nerves and he would come back around. But when she went into labor he was nowhere to be found.

There must have been hundreds of missed calls to the mystery man from Lucille's phone that were made by Patricia as the recent college graduate waited in the hallway with her boyfriend, James, during the delivery of her niece.

"His name is saved as 'babydaddy' in her phone," Patricia rolled her eyes as the last ring ended before the message for the voicemail box chanted its instructions in her ear once again.

Everyone was shocked by his audacity to go missing, especially after leading Lucille on to believe that he wanted this day to happen just as badly as she did. When he never showed up or returned a phone call,

Lucille accepted the fact that her heart and mind had been played with by a man who may have loved her once but certainly did not any longer. She found it difficult to love and appreciate this baby that she introduced to the world as Melanie Lucille Harper, sharing her father's last name as well as his big brown eyes.

Lucille thought Melanie was meant to strengthen her parents' love and bring them together forever in the bond of a marriage they had been planning for months, but she began to believe that Melanie may have actually been the cause of his disappearance. Or that her arrival revealed the fact that the father's intentions were never good, probably never truly loving Lucille or caring to have this baby in the first place. Maybe Melanie's birth gave him the most perfect and twisted reason to go missing and break away from a relationship he never intended to be in forever.

Lucille's mind was in the wrong place.

She viewed the blessing of Melanie as more of a curse, and she displayed the immaturity she had yet to grow out of when she decided she no longer wanted her.

The family collectively agreed that they did not want Melanie to be placed into the system and if Lucille would not take care of her, one of them had to. Lucille's parents volunteered to take Melanie in and raise her as their own, but Lucille would not allow it due to her claims that they could barely love her the right way and she would never trust them to raise her daughter.

Shannon was aware of the tense relationship between her sister and parents and as much as she did not want to do this she stepped in and took responsibility. Her commitment to being the big sister that hated to see her siblings down overpowered the fact that she and Mark never even wanted kids. She just needed to pull this family together as much as she could before they completely fell apart. And regardless of how frustrating Lucille may be, Shannon still felt the need to clean up her messes ever since they were younger, as well as make up for her own mistakes that she had made with Lucille in the past, feeling guilty for not being there to prevent her homelessness and drug use.

Lucille was grateful for Shannon's selflessness, once again, and was more than willing to transfer the weight of the baby, bundled in blankets, from her arms to her sister's. After she and the baby had been home from the hospital for a couple of months and everything was finalized, she moved out of Shannon and Mark's house to get her own place.

The years went by and Melanie grew into a beautiful little chocolate girl who was present for all major family events, unlike her mother, such as the wedding of her Aunt Patricia and James and the birth of her baby cousin, Tamryn.

Lucille was back at a distance from everyone and as bad as Shannon wanted to reach out to her again, she wasn't sure how to go about it without having to awkwardly introduce Melanie to her mother and face stumbling over words to answer the questions that would follow.

There were a couple instances that occurred every year or two where Lucille would pop up at Shannon or their parent's houses from time to time, but she never stayed around long and Shannon made sure to keep Melanie upstairs and out of view.

Lucille seemed to be in bad shape, but not as bad as the night Shannon had found her homeless and wild in the projects. She would give her big sister the same spiel about being okay and healthy and Shannon always pretended to believe her while knowing in her heart that Lucille was headed down the same road she found herself on before. Shannon wished that she could do more for her, so she bought a small cell phone for Lucille to use in order for the family to have a way to get in touch with her and vice versa.

You can only do so much for someone who doesn't want any help.

Lucille displayed her usual gratitude, "I love you, Shannon. I'm sorry I'm such a fuck-up," leaving out of the house with the phone clenched tightly and into the dark of the night, climbing into a van parked down the street. The brake lights flashed as the vehicle was placed into drive and Shannon's lost little sister was carried back to her destination of magical highs and damaging lows.

Melanie was good at pretending to be in the bed asleep when her mother made her surprise visits, but she was always sitting at the top of the stairs listening and wondering. She always battled with herself whether she should peek and get a view of this strange woman who seemed to ask a lot about her and only came to see her Aunt after the sun had gone down like she was a vampire. She never had the guts to risk giving up her hiding spot. So, she would sit there in the shadows of the upstairs hallway with her back against the wall and just listened. Their short conversations always left her Aunt

Shannon crying into her Uncle Mark's chest. Then she would retreat back to her bedroom and drift into a sleep that made the whole scenario feel like a figment of her childish imagination.

◇

Melanie and I grew older and she was never one to talk about her feelings regarding her mother and all that occurred, finally finding out everything at some later point in her childhood and me finding out from eavesdropping in my parent's conversations.

I could just see the differences between our situations and how hers could have had a negative effect on her but she never acted out the way you would think she would. She wasn't too emotional when it came to things, which could be odd for her being a young woman but she always preferred to keep her feelings to herself.

Melanie was pretty popular in high school but never did much to draw attention to herself, it just happened. She only really hung out with her best friend named Lance, who I could swear was in love with her but she was never willing to admit it. They were almost always together, studying for final exams, being each other's date for prom. He seemed to keep her focused on graduating and a smile placed on her face, but after she moved to California, she would only talk about him occasionally and then his name slowly stopped coming up.

I just assumed they did not have as much time to keep up with each other because of the distance.

The last time I even saw Lance was at Melanie's going-away cookout, which was also the last time I saw Melanie before she left.

◆

Aunt Shannon had that old soul music blasting from her stereo, her body moving to the beat as she laughed and played hostess. My dad joked how Aunt Shannon must be happy to be getting Melanie out of her house and my mother smacked his arm, playfully, holding in her giggles.

There was a decent amount of family and a couple of Mel's friends from school, including Lance. We were all packed in the small backyard of Shannon's house eating ribs, hot dogs, and other grilled favorites. Mel and I took our plates and sat on the steps of her back-porch away from everyone else. I can remember trying to piece the words together in my mind like a puzzle to ask Melanie how she could be so willing to move across the country and leave us all behind. She did not even know anyone in the state of California. Everything she had and ever known was right here in Ohio. I was sad to see her go, but it brought an unexplainable warmth into my heart to see her happy. It was a happiness that I had never seen her display before, and I was ashamed to admit that I selfishly found comfort and warmth in the thought that she would more than likely be back soon anyway.

How could she survive such a drastic move?

I took a bite of my hot dog and completed the puzzle of what to say, "Are you scared?"

"Not really," She was sitting on the step next to me, her two, long french braids tossed over her shoulders as she stared over at Lance dancing with Aunt Shannon. A smile crept upon her face.

"Why don't you want to stay here? I'm gonna miss you." I did not want to guilt Melanie into staying here with me, but I didn't want her to leave. I was thirteen at the time and having Melanie around as a sister-figure was a huge help during this hectic stage of puberty and confusion in my life.

"I just never felt like I belonged here. Aunty has her moments where she doesn't act like my landlord, like today... Lance is the best friend I could ever ask for," She looked at me and touched my arm, her hand surprisingly cool under the heat of the beaming sun and her nails manicured with bright pink gel polish, "And you... You are the best and sweetest little cousin ever. I just have this need in my heart for something. Like something is missing... So, if everything that I have is here, that missing piece must be out there somewhere. I know you may not understand right now, but one day you will."

One day you will.

I stared back at her and started to get that lump in my throat that always seems to form before the tear ducts open wide. My eyes started to burn as they built up with water so I fixed them back on my plate and took another bite of my hot dog to fight the sadness.

She was right. I did not understand at all. Maybe I wasn't like a little sister to her and she was only nice to me because I was a little girl. "What if it doesn't work out?" The words push passed the food stuffed in my mouth before I could hold them back.

"It's all in God's plan. I have a good amount of money saved up from wrapping all those burritos at work," She laughs, "And the lady who is renting the room in her house to me seems nice. We will see what happens."

"Is Lance sad? You know he loves you, right?" Melanie cuts her eyes at my comment, replacing a verbal response with a bite of Aunt Shannon's famous macaroni and cheese.

"You know I'm right!" I laugh, glancing at Lance just in time to catch his eyes on Melanie. Then he peers away, taking a seat with his plate of food at the table of other recent graduates from their school.

Melanie sighed, "He is not in love with me. You watched too many Disney movies growing up, kid. And no he's not sad, he is happy for me. As you should be too."

Two days later, she drove her 1997 Honda Accord across the country. Our constant contact with each other reassured me that she truly did love me like a sister and we watched each other grow from a distance. I had a front row seat to the *Melanie Harper Show* as she

AWAY

became a beautiful and resourceful woman. She left the place she felt she did not belong and never looked back. Then successfully found the home she had been searching for. Now here I was, fresh off the plane ready to call her home my new home as well.

◆

Back to the LAX terminal, I grabbed my phone out of my purse and tapped "MELANIE" so it would dial her line, catching the time displayed on the screen at "3:48 PM". I told her my plane was landing at 3:25 PM and the terminal, but I just realized I don't even know what kind of car she has for me to watch for her arrival.

How did I forget to ask that?

The phone rang a couple times then went to voicemail. Is she running late? Did she ignore my call? Shit, did she forget?

My eyes scan the terminal for a bench to sit down at.

This suitcase is heavy. This carry-on is heavy. This purse is heavy.

It's eighty-four degrees and I have on an oversized Ohio State sweater and a red infinity scarf.

Hey, look! She must be from Ohio!

I find an empty spot next to an older woman and head over to take some of this weight off of my body. The woman glances at me as I sit beside her and I smile. She smiles and looks away. I glance back at my phone.

3:52 PM.

"Where are you from?" The woman's face is still facing the opposite direction, but she is clearly addressing me.

"Cleveland... Ohio."

She turns and looks at me, the wrinkles on her tanned face are minimal until she smiles, "You look like a young woman on a mission."

I raise an eyebrow and look down at my outfit; big sweater, black Vans sneakers, jeans, and I can only imagine how ruffled my hair looks. I think I look like a young woman that's been on and off of airplanes all day. "What gives you that impression?"

"I can just see it."

I glance past her to let the discomfort of her response ooze off of me.

Maybe it's the scarf.

AWAY

The woman gets up from the bench, "I hope you find what you are searching for, sweetheart." She walks away, down the terminal and out of sight.

There goes the first person I met in L.A.

As I was staring down the terminal and the woman left my view, a black Range Rover with black rims and the darkest tinted windows pulls up in front of me. The passenger side window rolls down and there is Melanie's screaming face.

"Taaaaammmmmm! My baby cousin!" She jumps out of the car and runs over.

Melanie's brown skin glows in the sunlight and those big, brown eyes shine with joy. She also has a curvaceous body that attracts the attention of a couple other returning travelers.

Small waist, thick hips and backside.

Her hair also changes almost as often as her panties and right now it is styled in a cute jet black bob haircut.

She looks gorgeous, the best I have ever seen her. Judging by her smile and excitement running over to me, she is just as happy as the day of her going-away party eight years ago, if not happier.

I smile and get up to grab my bags. Bending down and swinging my carry-on over my shoulder, the movement is interrupted and I lose my grip as Melanie wraps my body up into the embrace of a tight hug.

We are screaming and spinning in circles and the brief glimpses I can see of the faces surrounding us tells me that everyone is enjoying our reunion almost as much as we are. I laugh and almost cry, still in disbelief that I am even here. It has been years since we have been in each other's presence and while video messaging is awesome, it could never compare to this.

"I can't believe I'm really here with you right now!" We finally stop the hugging and spinning and I reach back down to grab my bag again, placing my other hand on my suitcase.

She grabs the bag out of my hand and places it back on the ground, then removes my other hand off of my suitcase and interlocks our arms, "You should let someone else take care of that stuff", she says, and at that point, I notice the man who was driving the truck has gotten out.

He was standing there watching us with the most beautiful smile. At about 6'3" tall with a light-brown complexion and a wavy hair cut, wearing a white v-neck underneath a white blazer with white dress pants, black loafers, and black sunglasses.

Look what God did.

He opens the back of the truck and comes over to grab my things.

"Tam, this is my good friend Ronald. Ronald, this is my favorite baby cousin Tamryn," Melanie smiles at him then looks back at me.

He puts his sunglasses on his head, revealing sparkling light brown eyes, and he smiles as he picks up my bags, "Welcome to California, Tamryn. I know Melanie will take very good care of you... I'll be sure of it", his voice is deep but sweet and he goes to place my bags in the trunk.

I look at Melanie and she winks at me.

"Come on, get in let's go get some food!" Melanie leads me to the luxury vehicle, "I am so happy you're finally here! Are you hungry? How was the flight?"

My answers to her questions are delayed as I climb into the nicest backseat I have ever been in. There is tan leather interior and black floor mats that are either freshly vacuumed or fresh out of the store. Screens are built into the back of the seats and a huge screen is located on the dashboard, currently displaying the title of a song playing on satellite radio. The new-car smell fills my nostrils, urging me to take several, subtle deep breaths.

Who is this Ronald character? What does he do? How does she know him?

Pause.

Who cares? I just landed in L.A. and was picked up in a Range Rover. I am basically a celebrity already.

Ronald gets back in the driver's seat, clicks his seatbelt, checks his mirrors, and we pull off from the airport to make our way into the city.

"I am a little hungry. My flight was okay, I slept the whole time. I almost thought you forgot about me back there."

Melanie turns around in her seat to look me in the face, "I would never forget about you! Ronald drives like he's eighty years old!" She taps his shoulder flirtatiously.

A smirk appears on his face, "Don't try to blame this on me, you're the one who took forever at Tiffany's... Give her the gift."

Excuse me?

My eyes widen. Tiffany's? Give who the gift? Little ol' me?

AWAY

As if letting me come stay with her isn't enough. I'm so excited and I just can't hide it. I might pee. But, all I manage to say is, "Gift?"

Melanie gives Ronald a stare so cold it would have frozen him if it wasn't so hot out here, "Way to ruin a surprise you ass." She turns back to me, "I would give it to you now, but I want to give it to you later," She winks again. "I want In-N-Out. Do you like burgers?"

I haven't had a burger since my family's Labor Day cookout, but I heard In-N-Out is pretty popular out here so, "Yes, I love burgers!"

Melanie smiles, turns back around in her seat and cranks up the radio. Reggae music blasts through the speakers.

I bob my head to the beat and pull out my phone to text my mother, *I made it. With Mel now. Love you.*

Determining that the tint is too dark to truly take in the views of these west coast streets, I press the button to roll my window down all the way.

Ronald takes notice and lowers their front windows followed by opening the double sunroof. I smile.

I cannot stop smiling.

My phone vibrates with my mom's response, *Good. I love you too. Call me later.* I close my eyes as the breeze blows throughout the truck and brushes across my face. Then I open them back up to the beauty of my new city.

I made it. I am here.

I set my mind to a journey and it has officially begun. I am embarking on a search to reveal exactly who I am and while I am not sure what I will find or where I will end, I am ready.

Three.

Los Angeles, Present Day

Stuffed and satisfied stomachs.

From the burger place, Ronald drove us back to Melanie's loft in West Hollywood. The outside of the building is so clean and contemporary, the sun dropping lower in the sky reflecting its light off the huge windows. The small line of shrubbery surrounding the perimeter separates the building from the concrete sidewalk and is manicured perfectly. All of the elements of the apartment complex scream prestige, with a soft whisper to make it clear, *You have to have a lot of money to live here.*

We pull up to the entrance of the parking garage underneath the building and Melanie hands Ronald her access card to swipe across the monitor. It blinks green and the gate opens, so we head into the garage, the light from the late daytime sky being replaced by the dim lighting beneath the ground.

Ronald parks his blacked out Range Rover in a corner away from any of the other cars, and immediately gets out to grab my bags out of the trunk. I climb down from the truck and swing my casual purse back over my shoulder as Melanie interlocks her arm in mine, and we walk to the glass doors located just a few steps away that open to the elevators.

Melanie swipes her access card across another monitor and presses the "up" arrow on the touch-screen after the green blink of approval. I watched the display as both elevators raced down to obtain the calling resident, "4... 3... 2... 1... L... G".

Ding!

The silver doors of the hoist I am standing in front of slide open, revealing the spotless interior with the top half of the walls covered with mirrors. The first thing that caught my eye was my own reflection staring back at me. Here I am, equipped with the mess of my black, curly hair begging to be tamed and the slightly smeared eyeliner under my eyes.

Not as bad as I was expecting.

My short height of 5'0" is emphasized being sandwiched between Ronald who is over six feet tall and Melanie who is 5'5".

I look like their daughter.

And my straight body shape appearing drastically boring next to Melanie's doesn't help much. I have never been a self-conscious female, but the sight of her butt compared to my own has me wondering if mine deflated from sitting on aircrafts all day.

We step into the elevator and I stand behind Ronald and my cousin to quietly analyze the subtle curves of my body in the mirror.

Melanie presses 4, bringing the silver doors to a close and sending us up from the garage level as I stand on the tip of my toes lifting my huge sweater to get a good view of the reflection of my backside.

Okay, baby does still have back. Baby's back just looks childish next to Melanie's. That's all.

Melanie's eyes are glued to the smart phone in her hand, "My apartment is on the top floor. The only thing above us is the rooftop patio that no one has even been using lately."

Her voice startles me from my awkward examination in the mirror and I turn my head to face the front of the elevator in her direction.

Why would no one use a rooftop patio?

She reads my mind, "You may think it feels great outside, but these winter months are a little cooler than usual for people around here."

The doors open with their signature *ding* and I follow Melanie down the hall with Ronald trailing behind us, still managing to maintain his smooth composure rolling my purple suitcase atop the patterned tan, red, and blue carpet and my pink carry-on bag thrown over his shoulder. His shades remain resting on top of his head.

We get to the last unit down the hallway with 424 marked on the tan door in silver numbering. Melanie swipes with a different access card, obtains the green blink, and opens the door.

I am immediately stunned.

Vaulted ceilings. Numerous floor-to-ceiling windows allowing the natural light of the setting sun to illuminate in the last daylight moments. Modern white and gray décor. There is even a black, steel spiral staircase located in the back of the living area between two hallways that leads to a small loft I see from the doorway.

I walk to the middle of the room, pausing to take in the unexpected glamor of the scenery.

AWAY

How can she afford such a luxurious place? I never knew she was living like this. I was fully prepared to move out here and be cramped in a studio apartment where I would have to sleep on a pile of blankets on the floor.

"Welcome home!" Melanie skips into the house and throws her arms in the air as if I have just walked into my very own surprise party, and that is almost how I feel.

"I don't even know what to say. This place is beautiful, Mel. It must cost you a-"

"Thank you," She interrupts with a prideful smile spread across her face, "I'm just glad you like it. Ronald, can you please take her bags into my bedroom, love?"

"Of course babe," Ronald rolls my suitcase down a hallway that leads to the west end of the apartment.

Melanie grabs my hand, "Let me introduce you to my roommate, Sabrina," and leads me down the other hallway that leads to the east.

There is a door slightly cracked open at the end of the corridor and a closed door to our right with the light from inside shining through the bottom. Melanie knocks on the door that is cracked open and a few seconds pass before footsteps can be heard coming closer.

The door is opened wider and Melanie's roommate appears in the opening.

Sabrina has hazel eyes that are currently a glowing green with brown undertones, small freckles splattered around her nose and cheeks, and her skin is a lighter, tan complexion.

Her long, straight brown hair is pulled to one side and flowing over her shoulder which is covered with a blue UCLA hoodie with matching blue shorts and gray ankle socks. She has an ageless physical appearance, being the same height as myself with a baby face, but her mature demeanor leads me to the conclusion that Sabrina must be around Melanie's age.

She looks at Melanie, then at me, then back to Melanie and smiles. "Hey, M... This must be Tamryn," She says with a slight Spanish accent, reaching her hand out for me to shake, "I'm Sabrina. So nice to meet you."

"Nice to meet you too."

The toilet flushes from behind the closed door, followed by the sound of water pouring from the bathroom sink.

Melanie glances in the direction of the sound and then back to Sabrina, "Well, I just wanted to introduce you two. We won't hold you up. Sip some wine with us later," She turns and starts heading back down the hallway.

"Sure, if I finish this studying. First week of classes and I already have assignments due," Sabrina rolls her eyes.

I turn to follow my cousin back down the hallway to the living area and once we are almost there, I hear the bathroom door open behind me. I glance over my shoulder just in time to see the mysterious figure's muscular bare back and black basketball shorts as he shuffles into Sabrina's bedroom and closes the door behind him.

Hmm.

We turn the corner into the living room to find Ronald sitting on the sectional staring up at the mounted flat screen TV on the wall above the fireplace.

Melanie plops down on his lap and I walk over to one of the huge windows to check out the view.

"My little cousin has had a long day. We're going to relax and catch up a little bit," Melanie says in a soft voice followed by a kiss on Ronald's cheek.

I am staring out the window toward the end of the street, which runs out of view and into hills sprinkled with beautiful houses. The backdrop of the sky, painted with a confusing mixture of purple, red and orange is amazing.

I grab my phone to take a picture.

"Yes, your little cousin did have a long day. I'll let you get her settled," he taps Melanie's leg and she stands up. Reaching her hands out, he lets her pull him off of the couch and heads in the direction of the door. "Nice meeting you, Tamryn," He smiles at me as he moves his sunglasses from the top of his head to their proper position upon his nose.

I smile back, "Same here."

He looks back at Melanie as he opens the door, "Text me babe," and he walks out.

"I definitely will," she waits a few moments and I watch as she stares down the hallway before she hesitantly closes the door as if she misses him already.

"He is very sweet," I say, hoping my words encourage her to give me the scoop on their relationship since she hasn't mentioned anything about dating to me recently.

"He is. Come on back to my room and let's get you settled in," She heads down the west hallway and I follow after her.

I guess I'll get the scoop later.

Since their apartment is the last unit on this side of the floor, it is also a corner unit. With Melanie occupying the west end of the apartment, she gets to enjoy the luxury of floor-to-ceiling windows on two of the walls lining her bedroom. Her queen sized bed is placed in the corner where two of the huge windows meet, allowing her to take in the lavish sights of her neighborhood the moment she opens her eyes every day.

There is also a futon on the other end of the room against one of the internal, windowless walls and her walk-in closet is on the other side of one of her wooden dressers that stand between it and her bedroom door.

Ronald left my bags by the futon so I have claimed it as my "area" in her bedroom. This is much better than a pile of blankets on the floor.

Melanie gave me a tour of her decent sized bathroom and the linen closet located inside of it, handing me a towel to shower and leaving me to wash off my travels and get comfortable.

Feeling the hot water rush through my hair and massage my skin resulted in spending the duration of the cleansing immersed into deep thought. Even after the soap, shampoo, and conditioner long washed away, I remained standing and staring into space about the new start that lies ahead of me.

I have always been an extremely observant young woman to the point where it can appear creepy, and always tended to explore past the literal of actions and situations to make sense of their symbolism. Can it be safe to say that this shower signifies the washing away of an old routine to prepare my life's slate for a fresh, new start?

Maybe.

The steam fogs up the mirrors and the tan walls perspire.

I eventually stop encountering a dozen scenarios in my mind of what happens next for my future and step out of the marble tub to land back into the present.

After getting myself dried off and leaving my hair wild to air-dry, I throw on a plain, black long-sleeved shirt, black joggers, and my favorite black and white Nike sandals feeling thoroughly refreshed.

Returning back to Melanie's room, she is waiting for me lying on top of her bed in the dark, the only light of the room coming from a hint of the streetlights four stories below us and the screen of her phone. She looks up from her device, "Want to go on the roof?"

The view is beautiful.

The building isn't that tall, so it wasn't like I could see the whole city of Los Angeles, but it's the Hollywood Hills that keep getting to me. Seeing those speckles of light from those huge houses on the cliffs is captivating.

But it could have been a mixture of the sight and the way it got my mind going.

Just the thought that I could be up there one day, looking down on the city thanking God that I made it. That everything I did was not pointless and amidst the confusion of growing pains, I successfully found my calling.

I couldn't stop staring.

The rooftop patio of Melanie's apartment complex was equipped with a fire pit in the middle, surrounded by cute wooden outdoor couches styled with plump, tan cushions and pillows that line the fence wrapping around the perimeter of the rooftop. Christmas was a couple weeks ago, but there were still lights hanging and a tree decorated with a glowing white star on top on the far side of the patio.

Melanie threw on a pink sweater with her black leggings and carried the Red Berry Ciroc liquor bottle that had been finished off long ago, its contents replaced with a white strawberry-lemon Sangria that she had prepared, and I carried the wine glasses.

We had to be troublemakers and flip one of the couches around so it was facing the edge and with our feet up on the fence, we sat, sipped, and talked.

Even though we remained close over the years, there was much to catch up on regarding the details of when she first moved. Melanie was never one to disclose her struggles to anyone, especially me, unless it could provide motivation for something I was going through. So, I was never aware of how severely tough it was for her when she arrived in Los Angeles eight years ago.

She explained how the first woman she stayed with only allowed her to rent the room inside of her house for a couple of months. She was applying for jobs but wasn't having much luck, so she was forced to utilize the few friends she had made around the city from being out and about.

AWAY

When her couple of months were up, she was going back and forth from one friend's house to another because she hadn't saved up enough to get her own place. She endured sleeping on piles of blankets laid out on hardwood floors and being locked out accidentally on several occasions. The soft seats of her Honda helped her make it through those nights.

The last friend she stayed with agreed to help her out for a month, but her jealous nature caused her to question Melanie when she would walk in and find her sitting on the couch watching TV with her boyfriend.

Melanie was aware that her options were running out, as well as her resources.

The money she saved was quickly depleting and she started contemplating the use of her last few hundred dollars to get her back to Ohio.

Then she received a call for a position as an assistant manager at a clothing store that she had applied for months ago. Hope returned, even though she knew if she was able to save every penny of every paycheck it would still be difficult to afford rent anywhere.

She needed more time.

After a couple weeks in her new position with only a couple weeks left of finding a new place of residence, she met a customer at her job who was very interested in her. This man was dressed very well with eyes she characterized as sparkling with a remarkable vision. He used the explanation of his success in party promotion and his purchase at the store earning her a huge commission to market himself to her.

"Come see how I live," he said, inviting her to an event he happened to be throwing at a popular venue that night. So, Melanie told a couple of her co-workers and they decided to check it out.

He thought she was gorgeous, but he also took notice in her intelligence and charisma, so he ended up recruiting her to be a part of his promotion team.

Melanie started making hundreds of dollars just by telling people about and attending parties almost every night of the week. She was forever grateful to the gentleman that brought her on board, buying her the time that she needed. They became close, and he allowed her to stay with him for as long as she needed until she could get on her feet.

With the promotions and management position, it only took a few months before she had enough money put aside to afford a place that she could call her own. After a Craigslist search and a quick screening through potential roommates, she found the advertisement for the one she would decide to live with... Sabrina.

Melanie had nothing when they moved into the loft apartment in West Hollywood, but Sabrina did not mind providing everything from furniture to cooking utensils since she came from a pretty wealthy family. Her parents took pride in being able to spoil their only daughter, so the rent was paid in full for the first year of their lease. This also happened to be Sabrina's first year in college, so their generosity allowed her to make school the primary focus, as well as helping Melanie save up incredible amounts of cash and sell her Honda to purchase her first brand new car.

Sabrina and Melanie may have been aspiring toward different goals, but they clicked like the attraction between negative and positive charges.

Melanie has an extremely easy-going personality where she goes with the flow of almost anything. She does not intend to further her education, but is solely focused on the promotional company that she started entitled *SHE Inc.* The excess money she was able to save allowed her to hire ten beautiful women whose ages ranged from twenty-one to thirty years old. The women joined with the initial purpose of being a hot new promotional group that was bringing something new to the city, but they soon noticed the influence they could have on women from all over and the mission was expanded. In addition to marketing and attending the hottest clubs every weekend, they participated in charity events and spoke to young girls about preparing for their futures, as well as to grown women about not letting the past affect their goals.

It could be safe to say Melanie's tendency to avoid over-thinking has allowed her and her company to be completely successful so far.

Sabrina, on the other hand, is in her last year of undergoing a rigorous graduate school program to become a lawyer while she holds an assistantship with an esteemed firm in downtown Los Angeles. If she is not at class or working, she is in her bedroom studying or with her boyfriend whom she has been dating since she was sixteen. She would probably be as easy-going as Melanie, but her biggest goal in life is to impress her family who places a great deal of expectations upon her. Sabrina's father being a surgeon and her mother being the best Prosecutor in the region.

"*To whom much is given, much is tested*" and the last thing she will allow herself to do is fail.

Melanie and Sabrina both have strong ambitions as well as being business and achievement-oriented women, so they usually tend to be on the same page and can understand what the other may be going through. It also helps that their apartment is so spacious, giving them their own separate wings of the unit with private bathrooms. They don't get in each other's way that much.

My mind flashes back to the semesters I survived living in dorm rooms the size of Melanie's walk-in closet and I shudder from the thought.

"Wow, Mel... It truly amazes me how you really came out here and made all of this happen," I said, "I couldn't be anymore happier for you."

Melanie takes a sip from her glass and pats herself on the back, "Thank you, baby girl. It was all about staying patient and building the connections."

"So, what happened to the guy that introduced you to the party hustle? Is he upset that you started your own group?"

"Not at all. He actually owns a few clubs around the city now and is branching out with his own brand. He says I played a huge role in the progression he has attained and he actually returned the favor by helping me start my group," she smiled, "You met him... It's Ronald."

I definitely could have guessed that, but it was so obvious it went over my head. Perfect opportunity for a second attempt at getting the scoop on their relationship, "So he is just a business partner, basically?" I sip my wine and watch my cousin from the corner of my eye.

"Hmmm, a little business and pleasure," Melanie laughs. "Honestly, he means so much to me I couldn't fathom risking our relationship by actually dating him."

"So he wants to be with you, but you don't want to be with him?"

"I'm just not ready."

I take another sip. It may be beyond my brain capacity to understand what could keep her from being ready to be with a man who seems to care a boatload about her and has done so much for her. And he is insanely good looking! Yet, my mind cannot help but to wander back to one other thing, "Do you still talk to Lance?"

Melanie releases a small giggle stemming from the mention of a distant memory and I grow overwhelmed with curiosity, "Why are you giggling? He finally admitted his love for you, didn't he!!!?"

The small giggle evolves into a complete screech of laughter that escapes her lips and she struggles to hold her glass of wine upright as her body shakes from the humor that is unbeknownst to myself. I stare at her with wide eyes, assuming that the premature realization of preteen-Tamryn may have been right in allowing her love of Disney movies to predict the secrets of their friendship.

My cousin finally pulls herself together and musters the words, "He did end up telling me he always had feelings for me, goofball. Even though I was on the other side of the country he wanted to give a romantic relationship with me a chance."

"And you didn't do it!?"

"Hell no, I didn't do it! He may have been ready to work through the distance but I was NOT. It would have just ruined our friendship."

"Darn it, Mel." Happy ending ruined. "What if he would have confessed his love for you while you were still in the same state?"

Melanie stares out into the night sky, a look of concentration yielding her face as she squints her eyes in thought, "Probably not. I wasn't ready for something serious back then."

"Oh, gosh. Apparently, you're just never ready." I roll my eyes, playfully.

"You might be right… Let's just blame my 'daddy issues'," Melanie jokes. Her straight face giving a hint of seriousness, "But, honestly, everything happened the way it happened for a reason. There are no hard feelings between Lance and I. According to social media, he is living quite nicely as a financial advisor with a fancy corner office." She reaches her glass to me for a toast so I extend the hand out that is holding my glass, "I may not be in the corporate world, but I like to think I'm not doing too shabby my damn self." We tap our glasses with a musical *clink* and simultaneously take a sip.

The corner of my lips bend upwards in a slight smirk and I glance back in the opposite direction towards the hills of twinkling houses, "You're right."

The sound of her moving around draws my attention and I turn back to my cousin to find her reaching for something over the side of the couch. She sits back up and hands me a light blue bag with "*Tiffany & Co.*" printed in black lettering on the front and white handles.

Oh, goodness.

I had completely forgotten about the revealing of my surprise during the ride from the airport earlier, so my look of shock was as genuine as the surprise hiding under the white gift bag paper. I took the handles into my hand and peeked inside.

"I just want you to know that when I say I am happy you are here, I am truly happy you are here. I never really feel close to anyone, but you've always been like my baby sister. I know you have big goals and dreams and I know you are searching for more to life. Even though you are unsure of what that may consist of, I am so proud of you for wanting more than contentment. I have watched you succeed in everything that you do, and even when your efforts started to slip when you weren't as happy with school and where you were headed, you opted to make a huge change instead of standing by and complaining. I didn't have a support system like the one that you have when I was unsure of where moving would land me, so I'm glad to be able to be here for you and I know that no matter what you do, you'll be great, Tammy bear."

Don't cry, Tam, don't cry! If you do, you won't be able to stop...

I fight the tears as I reach inside and pull out a white gold necklace with a clock pendant.

"You have as much time as you need in order to find your way and I'm rooting for you." Melanie places her manicured hand on my arm with sincerity in her smile, "Was that a little corny?"

We laugh and I reach over to hug my cousin as the first tears fall, "No, Mel, not at all... Thank you so much."

I have inspiration sitting right in front of my face, letting me know that my purpose will be found. It is only my first day in this new city and I can already feel the positive influence of my new surroundings.

The hope and opportunities.

The *living* as opposed to merely *existing*.

The support is real. Melanie is rooting for me. My parents have faith in me. The inanimate houses in the hills are even fueling my motivation.

I can only go up from here and it is up to me to determine my destiny. I am completely prepared for what is in store for me.

Four.

Cleveland, 1997

It was almost as if the sky knew it was one of the more sorrowful days.

The sun was hidden behind thick, dark gray clouds and there were subtle rumbles of thunder that served as threats of another storm brewing.

Cleveland was welcoming the spring season with its arrival comparable to a lion's roar and it came bearing the gifts of a constant abundance of showers. The grass was still wet from the earlier downpour, causing muddy patches for the family to hop over and dodge like obstacles in a course as they walked across the cemetery to the burial location of Mark Williams.

They gathered around with their hands joined in solidarity and prayed, hoping a higher power would listen to their requests for comfort and strength as they prepared for the lowering of the casket into the six-foot deep hole.

Melanie glanced up at her Aunt Shannon and watched as she brought a tissue to her swollen, red face full of tears and patted gently.

At the tender age of eight years old, Melanie held her aunt's hand as her uncle's body was lowered into the ground. She glanced over to her Aunt Patricia whose arm was wrapped around Aunt Shannon's shoulders as she attempted to console her the best she could. Right beside her was Uncle James, her husband, who was holding their daughter and Melanie's three-year-old baby cousin, Tamryn.

Melanie loved watching Tamryn grow up, remembering the first time that she met her, when she was just a few days old and fresh out the hospital:

"Do you want to hold her, Mel?" Aunt Patricia smiled as she walked over to Melanie with the baby girl wrapped in a cocoon of blankets and nestled in her arms.

Melanie's eyes lit up and a huge smile formed across her face as she dropped her *Cabbage Patch Baby* to the floor and reached out her arms in anticipation of the real deal.

"You better not do that to my daughter!" James exclaimed, filling the whole room of family with laughter.

Patricia showed Melanie how to hold her arms and properly support the baby's head as she passed Tamryn down to her, "Perfect, there you go... You got it... Keep her head up."

Melanie was deeply intrigued by this little person.

This little person who was immersed in a peaceful sleep.

This little person who has been blessed with such loving parents that kept her surrounded by so much care and attention.

Shannon and Mark never treated Melanie badly, just never made her feel like she belonged with them. She knew that they weren't her parents, but they did things that parents tend to do, such as take her to softball practice, cheer for her at gymnastics competitions, kiss away the pain of a scraped knee. Yet, she could hear their conversations in hushed tones where they discussed the burden of being able to afford her presence, which led to her Aunt's complaints of constantly being the one to fix her little sister's mistakes.

At such a young age, Melanie concluded that she was indeed, one of the mistakes.

This conclusion empowered her belief that the hospitality she was shown was forced rather than sincere.

Melanie looked at baby Tamryn and knew that the love radiating from Aunt Patricia and Uncle James would never allow her to feel like a mistake or a guest within the family. She will always have an unbreakable sense of belonging and Melanie wanted nothing more than to contribute to that.

The burial ended and the family made their way back to Shannon's house to eat and keep her company on this dreadful day. By the time they had arrived, the rain had yet to begin to pour, just drizzles that did not require umbrellas and the quiet thunder that continued to taunt the city.

Shannon was no longer crying. She was smiling and laughing with everyone breathing positivity into her cozy home with their celebrations of the life of her late husband, rather than dwelling in the sadness of his homegoing.

The adults were sitting around the dining room table cracking jokes and recapping memories of Mark, while Melanie and Tamryn played with dolls in the living room.

"Here, put these shoes on the doll, Tam." Melanie handed a little plastic pair of red heels to Tamryn to place on the feet of the Barbie she was holding. Tamryn gave it the best attempt that she could being a toddler, but struggled due to the shoe being backwards.

Melanie laughed, "No, like this," and she proceeded to put the shoe on the doll for her baby cousin. "Now you do the other one." She looked back at Tamryn to notice that she wasn't paying an ounce of attention to the demonstration, her eyes fixed on something behind Melanie's head.

"Tam? Do this shoe…" Melanie said watching her baby cousin's eyes stare past her. She had always been a quiet baby, but this creepy stare and silence was freaking her out. "What are you looking at?" Melanie turned around and met the eyes of a woman who was staring through the window straight at her, her dark brown face appearing pale and weathered away as if she was a ghost.

Melanie screamed, hopping up and grabbing Tamryn's little arm all in one swift response to the fear she just experienced.

The adults came running into the room with Shannon leading the pack, and immediately saw the woman as she started to back away from the window upon being discovered by all of them.

"It's Lucille." Shannon whispered with a shakiness in her voice, and she walked out the front door to meet the woman on the porch.

"Melanie, take Tamryn upstairs, please." Patricia ordered her niece hastily without taking her eyes off of the woman as she followed her big sister out the door.

Melanie heard her aunt's demand, but could not gather herself to move.

Lucille.

She could not shake the sight of the woman's face from her vision. The questionable intensity she felt in her stare.

Lucille.

Her mother's name is Lucille. Could she identify the woman she just witnessed as the woman who gave her up?

She remained paralyzed, holding Tamryn's arm as her mind raced quicker than the adults filing out of the front door.

Her heart was beating strong enough to break through her chest.

AWAY

The face in the window looked nothing like the images she was shown inside of Aunt Shannon's old photo albums. She had always appeared so young and beautiful with clear, glowing skin and her hair styled to perfection. Not this woman with her hair disheveled, clothes torn, and bags the size of suitcases underneath her creepy, bulging eyes, giving the impression that if she was not a zombie she had to have been extremely sick and on a straight and narrow path to becoming the undead a lot sooner than later.

Uncle James bent down and interrupted Melanie's pressing thoughts, "Mel, baby, please take my daughter and go upstairs right now. Go, go, go right now." He stood up and ran out the door to catch up with the rest of the family, his greatest focus being on making sure his wife was okay in this twisted turn of events on a day that is already so trying.

Melanie pulled an innocent and oblivious Tamryn on to her feet and led her to the staircase, her hand trembling with her baby cousin's small arm still wrapped within her grasp.

Tamryn managed to grab the Barbie doll before being forced from their play-area, and trying to grab the railing while holding the toy was overwhelming, so

Melanie grabbed the doll to allow the three-year-old to safely climb the stairs.

"Go up to my room and play with the other dollies, Tam, I'll be right behind you with this one," Melanie smiled reassuringly and Tamryn nodded before obeying her big cousin's command and making her way to the second floor of the house.

Melanie turned around and crept over to the side of the screen door to peek outside and listen to what the adults were saying as she catches another glimpse of whom her mother has become.

Her aunts and grandparents were now down on the front lawn with Lucille, while the rest of the family monitored the situation from the porch, including her Uncle James who was standing in front of the door, causing Melanie to stare through his long legs in order to see what was going on.

"What do you mean Mark died? Today?" Lucille's face was filled with shock as she was delivered the news of her brother-in-law.

"He passed away about a week ago, Lucille. The funeral was today," Shannon crossed her arms over her chest as she tried to keep her composure, "What happened to the phone I gave you? I have been calling you... We have all been calling you."

"Something happened. I can get it back... Something just happened." Lucille's explanation contained no concreteness, just hot air as her stuttering voice was filled with distraction and nervousness.

Tears began to run down Patricia's face, "Why are you doing this to yourself, Lu? Please, let us take you back to the center." James hopped down the porch steps at the first sign of his wife beginning to lose herself, wrapping his arm around her waist once he arrived to let her know he was by her side.

He was always prepared to be by her side.

Lucille wiped her eyes before any tears could be shown and forced a smile on her drugged out face, "Girl, I am okay... What are you even talking about? I'm okay... I will get better eventually... I promise, but for now I am okay... Really." Her eyes reddened as they swelled with salty tears that she refused to let fall down her face in front of her sisters.

Shannon reached out her hand, interlocking her fingers with the scarred and dry fingers of Lucille's, "I can only imagine the demons you have been battling... Not just right now, but your whole life. I want you to know that we love you." She gestures to their parents standing back by the steps of the porch, tears running down the face of Melanie and Tamryn's grandmother as she takes in what they have unintentionally allowed their daughter to turn into, "Mom and dad love you and they wish they could fix everything that happened, they just don't know what to say or do to get through to you... I buried my husband today, Lucille, and I just know that I needed you here. But not like this. Not like this anymore."

Lucille looked to her parents as they looked back at her with eyes of regret and mercy. Then she glanced beyond her parents, the distant cousins standing on the porch watching her, and through her sisters' who stood directly before her, making eye contact with the child she gave birth to just over eight years ago standing behind the screen door.

A pain impossible to describe struck her chest as she recollected the fear in the little girl's eyes when she turned around and noticed her staring through the window.

Why did she allow herself to be placed in this predicament? Why couldn't she possess the strength of Shannon and the kind heart of Patricia? Instead, she managed to be the cause of a despicable amount of pain for these people who have only wanted to love her.

She should have never shown up at her sister's house today.

She should probably stop showing up at her sister's house from now on.

She has let her family down too many times to risk letting them down again by making another promise she is not guaranteed to keep.

Shannon is right: There are demons surrounding her.

She sees them everyday, fighting the same battle over and over without a single victory under her belt. They have succeeded in obtaining her soul and do not plan on relinquishing their prize anytime soon.

She cannot keep bringing this around these people.

And she would not dare to admit the reason why she stopped by in the first place: Her need for money.

Lucille releases her shaking hand from Shannon's grip as she backs away towards the sidewalk, "I am so sorry about Mark, Shannon. I am so sorry about everything. I promise I'll get another phone." She knows the last part is a lie and judging by the look on her sisters' faces they are well aware of its false validity as well.

The clouds above them grow darker as the drizzles slowly evolve into a full downpour.

The storm has arrived.

Shannon and Patricia say their *"I love you's"* as they watch Lucille back away and turn around to run just a few houses down to a car parked across the street. As the vehicle drives off, the family begins to make their way out of the rain and back inside of the house, reminding Melanie of the orders she was given by her aunt and uncle.

She runs up the stairs just in time to hear the screen door open as everyone comes gathering back inside.

Tears of anger release down Melanie's cheeks.

Lucille.

The woman who did not want her. The woman who made eye contact with her twice and never made an attempt to speak to her. The woman who turned Melanie into "the mistake" and disappeared, ripping away any chance of her being a true member of a "normal" family since the one she was supposed to be a part of did not do a good enough job at hiding how difficult it was to have her around.

Now that her Uncle Mark was gone, all that she could foresee were matters becoming even tougher.

Her aunt was now faced with the burden of taking care of Melanie all alone and she worked enough hours at the hospital already.

Melanie had never been an emotional child, choosing to bottle everything up inside seemed to be the best option due to not feeling comfortable enough to express how she felt to anyone. The strength of the current emotion that she was feeling was overwhelming her to the core: Hate.

Five.

Los Angeles, Present Day

We went to all of the famous locations I had heard about or seen on television.

Lunch on Melrose. Shopping on Fairfax. Taking pictures from the car as we drove down Rodeo Drive in Beverly Hills. I knew it would be pointless to get out since I could not afford anything from any of the stores on that street.

Melanie cleared her schedule for the first few days of my stay. From the moment that we open our eyes in the morning to the moment that we close them at night we ran around the entire city as she gives me her own special tour.

We indulged in a great deal of people-watching as we walked down the Venice Beach boardwalk until the strong amount of salt water in the air caused our hair to frizz. My naturally curly afro became a nest of knots and tangles that I was able to pull back into a bun, but Melanie had to get us out of there before her bob haircut went wild because it is too short to pull back.

I convinced her to make our next stop Santa Monica Beach so that I could watch the sunset from the top of the Ferris wheel, so she grabbed an emergency baseball cap from her backseat and that is what we did.

There has always been something about sunrises and sunsets that fascinate me to the point where I always feel inclined to stop and stare. The world can be so magical if you allow yourself to enjoy its natural beauty. The simplest things can reassure you that your biggest decisions have led you to being where you need to be when you need to be there. It's just that when our minds are clouded with worry or stress, it becomes a lot tougher to take the time to pause and open our eyes wider in order to catch the right signs that can be found underneath our noses.

I have never felt so *right* in my life.

Ever since I landed, there has been nothing but good vibes. No stressing myself out over irrelevant matters or even worrying about my next moves and plans.

I am just living within the moment and enjoying the gifts to be found in the present. So far, that consists of the simplest joy of Melanie and I catching up and talking the way we always used to.

My body is still growing accustomed to the Pacific time zone, so I woke up around 6:00 A.M. this morning and just laid on my futon in Melanie's room.

Her light snores served as background noise to my thoughts as I stared at the ceiling while the sunrise crept through her closed white curtains. Flashes of pink and orange colors slowly brightened the room from one corner to the next.

I told myself that watching the sunrise from the rooftop would make for an amazing start to a day, so I made a mental note to make that happen before my body gets used to the time zone and I go back to awaking later in the mornings.

About an hour went by while numerous other tasks were listed in my head, as well as questions to ask Melanie about *SHE Inc.* and random thoughts about friends from back home until my mind finally decided to relax just enough for my body to drift back to sleep.

An undisclosed amount of time past before I was peacefully brought back to consciousness by a pillow bouncing off of my face, followed by Melanie's soothing voice. "Time to WAKE YOUR ASS UP, TAM! Breakfast is calling!"

She can be unbearably sweet at times.

It had just broken into the afternoon when we returned to the apartment from a quiet and chic breakfast spot downtown where the meals were known to be extremely delicious and plentiful.

I could feel a food coma approaching as we stepped into the living room. Melanie fell to one side of the sectional as I fell to the other and she asked what I wanted to do for the rest of the day.

"You're the tour guide," I began. "What should we do today? You know I'm down for anything."

Melanie pulls her phone out of the gold satchel placed beside her and taps at the screen. "Hmm. We can head over to Hollywood Boulevard so you can see the Walk of Fame and take a picture with a fake celebrity. That's one thing we haven't done."

"Okay, let's go." I began pulling myself off of the couch when Melanie raised her hand with strong opposition to my sudden movements.

"Wait, wait, wait. Give me about an hour. I need a nice long nap after that monster of an omelet that I just ate."

I laughed inside at the irony of her being just as tired as I am even though her sleep remained undisturbed at the crack of dawn while I laid awake and restless.

My butt lands back onto the couch and I wrap a black fur blanket that they had thrown over it around my body.

"You've had me all over the city these past couple of days! It took me about a year to do all of this stuff when I moved out here and you have me doing it in less than a week!" She tosses a black and white striped decorative pillow at me but this time I am able to catch it.

I toss it back towards her, completely missing my target and sending the pillow over Melanie's head and into the kitchen. It could be safe to say that I have gotten a little rusty with athletic activities since my volleyball days ended. "I just love it here so far. Thank you again, Mel... For doing this for me."

She continues to tap on her phone, "I'm just glad you're having fun, love."

"I am absolutely glad you ladies are having fun too." Sabrina walks into the living area from her hallway with a huge smile, picking up the pillow and tossing it back towards us as she heads into the kitchen.

She is wearing a long-sleeved, nude turtleneck tucked into a long green skirt fitted to her curves, a green fur vest, and nude pumps.

On her way to work as usual.

Her boyfriend emerges from the hallway after her, but this time his back is covered with a black t-shirt.

Melanie sits up to look over the couch. "Hey, Bri. Hi, Miguel," She turns back to me, "Tam, this is Sabrina's boyfriend, Miguel."

Miguel is about 5'11" with a lighter complexion and a curly haircut. His ethnicity appears to be a mixture of Caucasian and Spanish, but he does not have an accent like his 100% Latina girlfriend.

Melanie was just telling me at breakfast how he goes to UCLA with Sabrina while modeling on the side and plans to graduate in May with a degree in computer technology.

He is smart, handsome, and cheats on Sabrina like she is an exam that he did not study for.

There have been instances of his unfaithfulness several times over the span of their relationship. When they first got together as teenagers, news would spread around their high school like wildfire whenever he hooked up with a classmate at a house party over the weekend. Enough of those embarrassing events led Sabrina to give him her most precious treasure: her virginity. She did this in hopes that he would stop looking to get anything from anyone else now that he could satisfy all of his needs with her.

Wrong.

This school year alone, he has stepped out on her at least twice (*at least* being the most crucial of wording because who knows how many more times this has happened outside of Sabrina's knowledge). Out of all the women he could choose to cheat on his girlfriend with, he decided on a female that Sabrina had considered herself to be pretty close to.

Oh, *frenemies.*

So, why wouldn't Sabrina take into account how beautiful she is, and even regardless of her looks, come to the realization that no one should ever deal with a partner that blatantly disrespects them over and over again? It turns out Melanie asked her that exact question, which she also shared with me between bites of her omelet and my indulgence in the Belgian waffle that sat before me.

Sabrina has made the duration of their relationship her safe zone.

She finds comfort in the fact that she has grown close to such a handsome dog, who may stray from time to time but always finds his way back home to her. She does not want to start over with anyone else. She does not have time to start over with anyone else. Her family, who she keeps in the dark about his hurtful actions, absolutely loves him. And she uses her beauty to combat breaking free by claiming that she "is too beautiful to be alone."

Alas, Miguel's method to his madness does not exist.

Sabrina has possession of the key that could set her free from the constant exposure of heartache, but she drops it to the ground in order to guard her heart with excuses in a battle of "love" similar to bringing a knife to a gunfight.

Illusions versus reality.

Miguel has one hand on the strap of his book bag that is thrown over one shoulder and the other hand rests in the pocket of his blue jeans. He smirks before speaking, "What's up, Melanie? And nice to meet you... Tam?" He raises an eyebrow at my nickname.

"It's short for Tamryn... Nice to meet you too." I push the background story I was told regarding Miguel and Sabrina's relationship to the back of my mind.

"Hey, Tamryn... I've been meaning to ask you something." Sabrina walks around the black marble counter of the breakfast bar with a banana in her hand and twirls one of the bar stools to face towards Melanie and me before planting herself upon it. "Were you planning on working during your stay with us? I am just wondering because this apartment is so expensive and the extra help would be totally appreciated." She begins to peel her fruit and bats her long eyelashes as she waits for my response.

It could make sense that they would want me to help out while I am staying with them and finding a solid job could be a way to make my move more official. I just haven't put any thought into it yet. I have only been in town for a few days.

I look to Melanie, who is squinting her eyes at her roommate with a puzzled look on her face before she opens her mouth to respond for me, "Actually Sabrina, I was going to ask my cousin if she wanted to join my promo group." She spins her head back in my direction, "I wanted to ask you about it later but since it has become a concern, I may as well ask you now?"

Joining *SHE Inc.* definitely has the potential to be an awesome gig.

I remember seeing their pictures posted across Melanie's various social media accounts and reading small captions about the events that they have been a part of and the volunteer work that they have done. Yet, I never knew the extent to how successful the group was until she explained it to me the first night I was here. Working with Melanie as I get paid to party and model would have been enough to seal the deal with me, but they have so much more to offer than that which makes the opportunity all the more attractive.

My only concern is that this company is Melanie's *baby*. If I am unable to step up to the plate and fit in with the women that she strategically selected to make her business a success, I risk the awkward happening of being fired by my big cousin.

But then again, it could be safe to say that Melanie would never make a decision with a consequence of jeopardizing her money. So, if she is offering me a spot on the team she must believe I'll be an all-star.

I shrug my shoulders nonchalantly, as if the offer extended towards me did not warrant that extensive amount of contemplation, "Of course."

"Well, it suddenly appears that the job question is taken care of. Prematurely. But it is taken care of." Melanie turns towards the kitchen and Sabrina is halfway finished with her banana, a look of satisfaction on her face when she stands from the bar stool.

Miguel's text message alert breaks through the small moment of silence.

Sabrina's eyes shoot towards him as he unlocks his phone, then back towards us appearing distracted with a new concern. "Well, great. I'm glad that is settled. Time for me to head on out of here." She walks to her boyfriend and taps his shoulder as she tries to steal a peek at the screen of his phone before he swiftly tucks it back into the pocket of his jeans.

He winks at her.

She raises an eyebrow at him. "Let's go, papi."

They make their way towards the door after she informs us that she will be going to her parents' house in

Malibu for dinner when she gets off work and may stay the night at Miguel's house.

Miguel gives us a nod of goodbye as he follows out the door behind his woman and the sound of their footsteps fade as they get farther down the hallway.

"She can just be too much at times." Melanie sighs as she lies back down, grabbing the black and white striped pillow off of the floor and placing it over her face.

"I see. She couldn't even wait a week before wondering if I'll be working. She almost made me feel like I'm a lazy bum or something."

Melanie moves the pillow off of her face and looks at me. "At least it's out of the way, I guess."

I think back to when Melanie explained to me how they are total opposites, yet they are able to get along quite well because of it. Sabrina may be a control freak, but I know how nonchalant my cousin is. Melanie may not have brought up the job topic to me for months even though she claims that she was already planning on asking me about joining her group. While I am okay with that, I am even more okay with the agreement we just reached.

If things were to not work out I could always find a job at a normal place on my own. That would make me feel even better because it would be something that I did without a handout from Melanie.

Or, I could go ahead and put in the extra effort right now.

They are letting me stay with them, my cousin is buying me expensive jewelry and making sure that this experience is everything and more than what I hoped for. Why not fill out some applications in addition to being a *SHE* representative? The least I could do is prove that I did not come out here to mooch off her and her money. The money that she apparently has a lot of.

"Thank you for letting me join SHE," I begin. "But I still want to try to get hired somewhere else, too. Like at a mall or something. I want to help out as much as I can."

The raising of Melanie's eyebrows fills her forehead with lines of surprise. "Well, okay. That's understandable. You can grab some applications while we're out and about today. And of course I wanted you to join the team. I have always admired your modesty, Tam. But bringing you into the business gives me a reason to dress you up and cake that face full of makeup," She laughs, "I've been dying for the opportunity to see how much more gorgeous you will be with a little highlight and contour, little Barbie doll."

I do like my face natural with eyeliner and lip gloss at most, but I haven't actually seen it fully done in order to have a preference. I am not the best at applying makeup and I have tried a number of different eye shadows that always seem to make my big, brown eyes appear dirty as speckles of glitter are splattered all over my face. My attempts at applying different lipsticks never appear to look right on my full lips, turning me into a replica of Mrs. Potato Head. I have even made attempts to wing my eyeliner to no avail, the hours of watching tutorials online proving to be no match against my pure lack of the necessary artistry skills.

The bottom line is that it never works out the way I would like for it to, so I thank God that my bare face is decent enough to appreciate and keep it moving.

Besides, I do like to remain modest but a part of myself cannot help but to think, *Stop acting like a child. You are not a little girl anymore and haven't been for quite some time. Get your makeup done the right way, turn some heads, and break some hearts. Why not?*

"I'm sure you'll make me flawless, Mel." I pretend to flip my hair, which is all piled back up on top of my head in a messy bun.

"Okay so, nap time?" Melanie asks as she grabs the other black, fur blanket located on her side of the couch and spreads it over her curled up body, "Then we can get back to your *fabulous L.A life tour.*" She flutters her hand through the air as if glitter and stars were spilling out of her pink, stiletto-manicured nails.

"Yes, nap time." I cuddle back under my blanket and turn towards the back of the couch where I look over it and see the blue sky through one of the extravagant windows. My eyes get heavy and I do a lot better at ignoring my racing thoughts than I did earlier this morning as the food coma swallows my body.

We changed clothes to leave the air conditioned apartment and enjoy the perfect weather of the day.

Melanie was wearing a long pink, halter top maxi dress with brown gladiator-styled sandals and I threw on a long tan sleeveless maxi dress that I have had since high school with black sandals. The blazing sun made it hot enough to be comfortable without sleeves while the soft breeze made the heat bearable.

We decided to catch an Uber ride to Hollywood Boulevard and walked a couple of blocks until we reached Hollywood & Highland.

I did have Melanie take a few pictures of me with fake celebrities, including an awesome impersonator of Michael Jackson and a perky TinkerBell. I also captured a number of selfies with the stars of real celebrities upon the Walk of Fame.

Then we grabbed some iced coffees and made our way through the outdoor mall. Our sunglasses perched upon the brim of our noses while we shopped and collected job applications for me along the way.

After a couple of hours, we bought some sandwiches and had a seat at an empty table to eat and rest our busy legs. The several bags holding our recent purchases of clothing and accessories were piled at our feet as I pulled the applications out of my favorite, white tote bag to start filling them out.

I figure I may as well get them done now, rather than relying on myself to get them done online later or to bring them back some other time. This area is so busy, filled with the hustle and bustle of all different types of people from all different walks of life, either ignoring the crazy characters lining the street or displaying their tourism as they take pictures and tip every single one. There are so many different movements and sounds such as dancing, singing, and even strong voices booming through megaphones about preparing ourselves for the end of the world.

It's all interesting to me right now, but I could see myself being annoyed by the manic energy if I have to come back to deliver these applications.

I could be ready to pull my hair out if I worked here every day.

But, it's the effort and willingness to do this that counts, so I dig a pen out of my purse and start writing. Plus, all of these stores probably get around thirty applications a day so what are the chances that I will actually be called for an interview?

The breeze is hitting just right, blowing Melanie's bob just a little as she sits with her legs crossed and the dark *Ray-Ban Clubmaster* sunglasses hiding her eyes. The view of her from behind my pink aviator sunglasses made me wish I had straightened my back-length hair and wore it down to feel the wind blowing through it. But,

AWAY

I left it in the wild bun which, surprisingly, adds a graceful touch to my exposed shoulders and gold hoop earrings.

Our sandwiches have been demolished and small conversations have come and gone.

I flip over the last application I have to finish, which happens to be for the shop that we purchased our iced coffees from, and start to fill in my references.

Melanie Harper. Former co-worker from campus food services job. High school volleyball coach.

"Wow, these ladies must be famous... Can I have an autograph!?" A guy laughs while walking over to us, flashing his gap-toothed grin while another guy follows behind him with a camera around his neck and a smirk on his face.

Melanie turns her head and peers over her sunglasses. Once she realizes that she knows the jokester she smiles and stands to hug him. "Oh, Jay... Your creepiness never ceases to amaze me."

I glance back at the guy with the camera and our eyes meet, the unexpected contact brings a nervous smile to my face. I move my sunglasses to the top of my head and look back toward my cousin while she reclaims her seat.

Jay laughs some more before glancing down at me, "Which friend is this, Mel? I don't think I've had the pleasure of meeting her." He reaches his hand out for me to shake and Melanie pushes down his gesture before I have a chance to act.

"This is my baby cousin, Tamryn. No touching." Her voice is playfully protective during the introduction. "Tam, this is Jay. Me and him have worked together on several gigs over the past couple of months and he is an hilarious and crazy pervert."

I smile and nod, "Wow, a hilarious and crazy pervert?"

"Ha! Your cousin is the crazy one and I'm definitely not a pervert. If anything I should be saying that about her..."

"ANYWAYS," Melanie interrupts, shoving Jay to the side and bringing his quiet friend to the center of our attention, "Who is this young man? You should take notes from him in learning how to keep your mouth closed!"

All eyes are on the camera guy as he licks his lips and looks back down to where I sit, forcing me to glance away before my face blushes and glance back when I hear his voice. "I'm Dylan."

And I'm in awe.

He had to be about 6'2" with a complexion comparable to caramel and thick eyebrows planted above his brown eyes that keep finding their way onto me. His hair is styled in a clean, tapered fade and a closely-shaved beard shadows the brim of his face. The black, short-sleeved button-down shirt that he is wearing looks great against his toned arms filled with tattoos, along with his black jeans, and Sperry boat shoes.

Simple and clean.

As much as I may be attracted to him, I have had my fair share of dating and regretful one-night stands during college, so I am not looking to start anything new with anyone. Not right now.

Even though I am almost close to reconsidering.

Almost.

"Nice to meet you, Dylan." Melanie says, reaching out her hand for him to shake.

Jay jumps back in front of Dylan and holds his arms out to the sides of his body as if he is guarding his friend from Melanie's hand. "Nope, don't touch!"

He bursts into laughter as Dylan and my cousin shove him back out of the way to formally greet each other, then Dylan turns back toward me with his hand reached out.

I place my hand in his.

Shake.

But when I attempt to pull my hand back he continues to hold on for just a second longer than the cordial act typically lasts.

Oh, goodness.

I look at Melanie and cannot see her eyes as they are hidden behind her shades, but I know that she is witnessing the moment.

My eyes glance up at his, which are squinting down at me in the sun while a smile shining with confidence is spread across his face.

He lets go.

I place my sunglasses back over my eyes with hopes that the pink tint will shield me from his charm.

"Are you ladies coming to my show tonight?" Jay asks.

"I didn't even know about it. Where?" Melanie responds.

"This venue downtown. It should be pretty cool, I'll text you the details. We have to get back to shooting these promotional photos for my next album, though. It was cool meeting you, young Tamryn." He does a salute towards us and starts walking away.

Dylan begins walking backwards away from the table, still looking at me. "It was nice meeting you ladies. I hope to see the both of you tonight." Melanie waves and I give a nod as he turns and follows Jay.

Melanie moves her sunglasses to the top of her head and burns a hole through my face with her eyes. "Dylan doesn't care about seeing US tonight. He wants to see YOU." She purses her lips together, holding in a smile, "He is definitely into 'young Tamryn' and 'young Tamryn' is definitely into Mr. Dylan the photographer as well! I noticed!" Her perfect white smile finally pushes through her lips as she teases and does the motion for quotation marks around the nickname Jay has given me.

I will not give my cousin the satisfaction of taking notice to anything. But I can feel myself blushing as I pick up my pen and look back down at the application still sitting in front of me.

Maybe if I just ignore her she will go away.

"Okay, you can try to act like you don't hear me but I'm not going anywhere. And neither is that little crush you seem to have," she points her finger in my face and laughs.

Okay, maybe she won't go away. Next plan.

"I do not have a crush, Mel. I don't even know him. He was just cute. It is not that big of a deal." I keep my head down and glance up towards Melanie, slowly.

She tilts her head but remains silent, watching me squirm as I try to find a way to get her off my back. "I'm not here for all that extra stuff, Mel. Guys aren't my focus right now."

"Okay, young lady. Whatever you say. He is a cutie, though. There is nothing wrong with expanding your focus. Just don't be too hasty with letting your guard down." She puts her sunglasses back on her face, sits back in the chair, and folds her arms across her chest.

Good, I think she is finished.

I look back down at my application and try to finish writing the information about my last reference.

"Why didn't we just have you do those online?" Melanie says as her phone vibrates from its position on top of the table. I ignore her, silently reminding myself that filling the applications out right now is better.

My hand hurts.

She reads the incoming text message before informing me of our new plans for the evening. "So, around 8 o'clock tonight we are heading downtown for

Jay's show. He just sent me the address. I won't even ask if you want to go because I already know you do."

I roll my eyes.

And Dylan's smile comes back to mind until I shoot down the thought bubble with the arrow of my reassuring thoughts, *dating would only be a distraction. Creating relationships with guys was the goal when you were in school, now the goal is creating yourself. Don't be dumb!*

After a few minutes, I finally finish the last application and we get up to do one more lap around the mall so I can return all of them to their rightful general managers.

Our Uber ride arrives around 5:30 P.M. to return us to the apartment and we squeeze into the backseat of the red 2015 Ford Fusion with our shopping bags.

"What does Jay do, Mel? What kind of show is it?"

Melanie is staring at her phone as usual, "Crazy Jay happens to be a crazily great singer. He's in this band called... Actually, I forgot its name. But their sound is a mix of soft rock, mellow Indie, and 90's R&B. I only show my face at these type of events to build connections and potential clientele, but this may actually be pretty enjoyable."

"Do you think you'll run into the coordinator of a high school program on self-esteem for young women at this concert?" I say with sarcasm and a playful smile.

"You never know what type of people you will meet, Tamryn. That's why you have to stay ready. You're not in Cleveland anymore. There can be a huge connection anywhere out here." She pulls a wad of business cards out of her purse, followed by a wink.

I analyze the interesting mix of music genres Melanie used to describe Jay's band and conclude that this may really be a cool show. Jay just seems so goofy that I cannot help but to imagine him being a stand-up comedian rather than a singer, so I am excited to see if what Melanie says is true.

I also must admit that I cannot help but to feel a little excited about running into Dylan again. It is obvious that he has an interest in me, and besides his attractiveness and confidence there is something else about him that draws me in.

A sense of mystery.

While I will force myself to avoid anything more than a friendship, I am faced with the need to know more about him. His essence has inflicted a bout of curiosity upon me and I am ready to feed it.

Six.

Los Angeles, Present Day

The large sign in front of the small, brick building has the black letters arranged upon the lit white background to read: *2NIGHT AT THE CRAWLSPACE - WIDE AWAKE & FRIENDS*.

"Oh, yeah! Jay's band is called *Wide Awake*. I knew it was something random that I would never remember on my own," Melanie points at the sign from her hand's position on the steering wheel and turns us into the parking lot.

There is a diverse plethora of people flooding the parking lot. They are different colors and sizes with numerous piercings, tattoos, and variations of hair color from neon green to jet black, and they are making their way to the doors of the concert hall from their parked vehicles.

The line of cars in front of us is slowly moving and beginning to extend behind us into the street. Everyone is in search of available parking spots in the crowded lot while simultaneously avoiding hitting the people. There are bodies everywhere cutting through the line of cars without any ounces of worry regarding being hit. Brake lights are forced to glow as cars are brought to immediate stops every time a person hops in front of headlights to run to the line at the door.

Melanie's car was not the only nice one in the lot, but many sets of eyes from the crowd were attempting to see through her dark tinted windows in order to figure out who occupies her silver 2016 Audi A6. My cousin's body language grows tense with every person who passes by.

"I don't know about having my car down here, Tam. Maybe we should've caught another ride." Melanie massages the steering wheel with both hands in an effort to alleviate her anxiety.

The line of cars can now be seen leading to the end of the lot where people are parking on the large yard of grass in the back of the building.

"Mel!" I gasped dramatically, placing my hand over my heart and startling Melanie, "Are you assuming by the looks of these people that your precious Audi may not be here when we come back outside? You shouldn't be so bourgeois." I laugh.

She shoots me a look of disdain.

We finally park all the way in the back of the yard, due to Melanie wanting her car to be as far away from everyone else's as possible.

The walk to the front doors of *the Crawlspace* is long, but we take our time as people walk around us, swiftly and filled with excitement.

Melanie's black single-sole heels *click-clack* with every step across the parking lot and she is wearing a white tank top tucked into her form-fitting dark blue jeans. A small black Chanel clutch detailed in gold is held at her side.

My outfit consists of a light blue jean shirt with the sleeves rolled up my arm about ¾ of the way, and I have it tucked into matching blue jean shorts with nude open-toed wedges strapped around my ankles. I decided to keep my hair in the bun with my gold hoop earrings which compliment my heels. My height is boosted and matching Melanie at 5'5", increasing the possibility that I may actually look my age tonight, instead of a high school girl.

Wishful thinking with this baby face.

AWAY

The line at the door was moving quickly and after only a few minutes, we were inside of the entryway to the venue. It smelled similar to an old basement. Four guards were checking everyone's identification and bags, as well as patting down the gentlemen for any dangerous objects that are not welcome inside of the building.

The place may seem run-down with scribbles of graffiti all over the chipped paint of the walls, but at least the owners are big on safety precautions.

I show my driver's license to one of the large, muscular men while Melanie hands her's to another as well as having her small purse checked. I move to the side and wait for her, my license and phone in hand while my chapstick and ten-dollar bill is squeezed into the pocket of my shorts.

The question of why I had not grabbed a small bag to carry my things suddenly dominated my mind as Melanie is handed back her purse and we take a couple more steps ahead to the ticket counter.

"Ten dollars." The girl behind the window says, followed by several pops of her gum and her finger twirling her long red hair.

"Each or for the both of us?" Melanie asks.

The girl gives a blank stare and Melanie's eyebrows furrow.

I reach into my pocket, but before I could grab my cash Melanie slaps a fifty-dollar bill on the counter.

The girl rolls her eyes as she grabs the money and slides two tickets along with Melanie's change under the window, "Enjoy the show."

The music grows louder as we finally walk into the concert hall and it's actually larger than I was expecting. The room is dark and spacious with the brightest lighting inside the building being used above the bar and the glowing lights above the stage.

Shadows of people are everywhere and different colored spotlights roam throughout the room, highlighting the smoke that can be seen rising into the air from many different areas.

The band that is currently performing fills the hall with a slow, ska-style song. Their lead singer is harmonizing lightly to the beat as she cuts her arms through the air in relaxed movements of dance with her eyes closed and long blonde dreads swaying from side to side with the rhythm of her body. She hits a high note as she reaches for the ceiling and the crowd goes wild for her talent.

AWAY

It is almost as if once we walked through those doors, we entered into another world. One with a population comprised of stoners and artists. The free-thinkers and rebels that don't feel inclined to fit in. Those who are deemed to be "outsiders" by the "normal" people who are afraid to confront them.

Yet, instead of feeling afraid while being in their midst I am complacent and intrigued. Who is to say that I could be classified as "normal" anyway? Especially when everyone's personal perception of normality varies, being surrounded by different commonalities and adhering to different standards. Even though I don't smoke, it may be coincidental that the people I would connect with the most in college were always high and always creating something. They seemed to understand me and the struggles I was having with my identity the most. I was always attracted to the bravery that they possessed to unapologetically, be who they are without a care of societal norms.

Melanie and I maneuver through the crowd with our arms linked and arrive at the bar as two girls were vacating their seats. A busy bartender greets us about thirty seconds after we sit down.

"Jack & Coke for me and… What do you want, T?" Melanie fingers through the money inside of her clutch.

"I'll have the same."

Our drinks are brought back to us in tall, cold glasses topped with cherry garnishes.

Melanie pays and hands me my glass.

I pull out my ten-dollar bill to give to her and she waves it away.

Expected.

So, I reach for my driver's license and chapstick to hand to her with the money so that she can keep my items inside of her clutch for safekeeping.

She is bound to forget that she has my things, so when I grab them out of her bag later I can leave the money, therefore paying her back without her being aware.

Plus, I can hold onto my phone but I would rather not risk losing my other belongings if they decide to slide out of my pocket in this dark, crowded space.

The girl with blonde dreads and her band finish their set and take a couple bows as they thank the audience and *the Crawlspace* for having them. They exit stage left and the host of the evening comes running out to take their place.

"Alright! Let's give another round of applause for Lisa Bean & the Cold Rabbits!" There are bursts of claps and whistles as Melanie and I give each other a mutual look of wonder and sip our drinks.

What is with the names of these bands?

"We are very glad to see that everyone is enjoying themselves! But, who's ready to see Wide Awake!?" He takes the microphone away from his lips to clap along with the crowd before yelling into it again, "I said... WHO IS READY TO SEE WIDE AWAKE!?" The crowd booms with claps and screams and I feel inclined to join, letting out a dainty "Woo!" and tapping my phone to the glass in my other hand gently in attempts of clapping with my hands full.

"That's better! Now give it up for your headliner this evening... WIIIIIIIIIIIDE... AWAAAAAAAAKE!" He replaces the microphone on the stand and runs off the stage as the lights above it go dark and the crowd goes wild.

There is the sound of a loud heartbeat blasting through the speakers as the shadow of a man walks out onto the stage and takes his place in front of the microphone stand followed by three other guys. One gets situated at the drum set, another is carrying a bass guitar, and the last one sits behind a keyboard.

The heartbeat fades out and there is a brief moment of silence, the only noise being sporadic screams of anticipation from within the crowd.

The first song begins with a soft melody spilling from the black and white keys underneath the pianist's fingers, followed by a beautiful and soothing tone erupting from the vocalist's mouth.

I look to Melanie and before I can even ask if that's Jay she nods her head yes.

The other instrumentalists chime in and I allow their music to make love to my ears. Every note that they hit from every strum of the guitar to tapping on the drums and the vocals escaping Jay's lips were right on cue.

Mental note: Ask Melanie where I can find more of their music.

The performance paired with the drink in my hand and even possibly the second-hand smoke I could be experiencing from people of the crowd forces me to submit to complete and utter relaxation.

My body sways from side to side upon my position on the bar stool and I close my eyes for a brief moment, taking in the lyrics:

"You are always near,

Your presence feeds me nightmares, yet

The dream is always sweet..."

The song comes to an end and the crowd erupts with cheers. There has to be screams coming out of every single person present in the building.

"Thanks for coming out, everybody," Jay says into the microphone. "We're gonna give you what you came for!" He is thrown back into his musical element as the drummer brings in the next song with a more upbeat pace and the crowd begins jumping up and down, waving their arms.

I look over and notice Melanie has finished her first drink and already holds the straw of a second one between her lips. A new glass ordered for me is waiting on the bar.

I finish off the last of my first drink and reach for the next one when a guy approaches Melanie and begins talking in her ear to combat the volume of the band. I glance back toward the stage and a flash from the camera of someone in the crowd sparks my interest, *where is Dylan the cameraman*?

I begin to scan the shadows of the room but I can barely see over the people who are standing right by us at the bar.

Standing on the base of my stool and being careful to balance myself, I glance above their heads. The hall is packed from wall to wall with bodies and all I could hope to do is recognize Dylan's frame or catch a glimpse of his face in the crowd.

Mission: Impossible.

I lean forward a little more and the back legs of my stool slightly lift off the ground, urging my reflexes to throw my weight back down onto the seat and grab a hold of the bar before the stool falls over and sends me crashing to the floor.

Melanie places her hand on my arm, "What are you doing?" she mouths and the guy she was speaking with remains by her side watching.

I lean in to yell in her ear, "I'm going to try to find Dylan so I can say hi!"

"Do you want me to come with you!?"

"No, don't let anyone take our seats! I'll text you when I find him!"

She grabs my arm again as I hop down from the stool, "Text me when you find him!"

I nod my head as the rush of alcohol from the strength of our drinks flows through my body in response to my standing. I almost buckle in my wedges.

Oh, crap.

I blink my eyes quickly hoping to make the buzz subside and give myself a moment to comprise a game plan before heading into the thick crowd.

There are a lot of people in here and Dylan is one person. Do I really want to find him to say hi? Would he even care if I did? He may be really busy taking pictures of the band.

Can I just stop psyching myself out so much?

I know that he would have to be close to the stage in order to get the best shots, so drink and phone in hand, I make my way through the maze of people in the direction of the front of the room. I try to squeeze between everyone as carefully as possible to decrease the chances of being bumped, spilling my drink or dropping my phone.

"Excuse me... Excuse me... Hey, can I get through here? Thanks... Excuse me..."

I finally make it extremely close to the front, only a couple more bodies standing between the stage and myself. Standing on the tip of my toes and being carefully balancing in my wedges, I am able to obtain a greater view of the people who hold the honor of lining the stage.

No Dylan in sight.

Mission: Failed.

So, I push myself to the very front figuring that I might as well enjoy the show since I have made it this far.

Jay is still foremost and center with both hands on the microphone stand and eyes closed, singing his heart out as the band plays along with his voice. I take a sip of my drink and listen as their sounds all cohere with one another, the shadow of someone on the left side of the stage consuming the corner of my view.

A camera is covering their face when I look, but once they move it down I am delighted at the reveal.

Dylan.

Of course I could not find him in the front of the crowd because he is taking pictures from the best location possible, the stage itself.

AWAY

Dressed in his all black outfit from earlier, he is able to blend into the background as he snaps away with his professional camera and moves around the group subtly, capturing the best images from every angle.

Jay has opened his eyes and is looking out into the crowd, taking the microphone off the stand and moving closer to the edge of the stage to interact with his fans.

He scans the front row and his sight lands on me briefly before continuing down the row then returning back to me. He winks with a smile when he notices who I am.

I wave.

He goes on singing his lyrics and looks over to Dylan who snaps a picture of the singer while he holds his attention. Jay points in my direction.

My heart skips a beat.

Dylan's eyes follow the guidance of Jay's finger and immediately land on me.

His bright smile glistens.

Jay continues performing and moving to interact with the audience, but I keep my gaze on Dylan. He motions for me to go around to the side of the stage by the access stairs before heading in that direction himself.

113

I make my way between the bodies of people and emerge from the crowd right by the stairs, meeting one of the large guards in charge of keeping people out of the restricted area.

Dylan is standing on a step behind the guard and puts his hand on the man's shoulder before leaning in to tell him something.

I watch Dylan's lips as he talks and after a few words the guard moves to the side and extends his hand to help me step up the stairs. Dylan takes my hand when I reach him and from there we go up to the stage, being careful to remain to the side and out of the audience's view.

Dylan's camera is attached to a black and white strap with red lining that he is wearing around his neck. He holds the device out of the way and reaches for a hug with his other arm. "I'm glad you made it," he says into my ear during our embrace, "You look pretty!" The scent of his cologne gently brushes by my nose. I inhale deeply.

"Thank you!" I say in his ear.

His arm is still wrapped around the small of my back and I turn around to face the band.

Peeking around the thin divider that separates the performance area of the stage from our hiding spot on the side, I look into the crowd to try and spot Melanie at the bar.

But she is not where I left her.

Our seats are now taken by two Asian women drinking martinis.

Where did she go?

I examine every face that I can see going down the bar to the back of the room and finally find Melanie talking and laughing at a table occupied by about four men, including the one she was speaking to earlier.

She reaches into her clutch and hands a business card to each one of the gentlemen.

Melanie definitely knows what type of strategies implement in her networking. She has always been naturally capable of working a room and gaining attention with her social persona. But, she also knows when using her looks can be equally, if not more beneficial in accessing the pull that she needs to build her brand.

If it works, why not do it?

I sip the last of my drink, which has been watered down by the melting ice inside of it and keep holding the sweating cold glass as I direct my attention back to the band's performance.

Dylan's hand grips a little tighter across my waist and an electric shock lights up my body from the unexpected squeeze.

I peek up at him from the corner of my eye to find his eyes on the band as he nods his head to the music. He must have felt me staring because he glances down, meeting my eyes for a split second before I avert them back to mid-stage.

He leans down, bringing his lips half a centimeter from my ear. "How do you like the band!? Pretty nice, huh!?" His cool, minty breath tickles the side of my face.

I turn my head, bringing my lips to his ear, "Yeah, they're great! I need a copy of their music A-SAP!"

"I'll make sure you get a lime snobby!" He smiles and looks back to the stage.

Pardon?

"You'll make sure I get what!?" I frown as a question marks fill my brain in trying to decipher his response.

Is it really this loud in here? Am I that tipsy?

The drummer bangs across his set during a solo that sends the crowd into heavy cheers. The building shakes, making it even more difficult to hear the words coming out of Dylan's mouth.

He tries again, "A shine Tommy!"

I shake my head and raise an eyebrow to show that I still don't understand.

Dylan grabs the empty glass out of my hand and places it on the floor, then takes my wet hand in his, leading me backstage.

We walk behind the black curtain serving as the backdrop for the band that has their "Wide Awake" logo plastered on the center in white lettering. I take a look around at the environment that is hidden behind the scenes. Its not as dark as the main part of the concert hall but is just as loud if not louder.

He leads me to a door marked with an "EXIT" sign above it in the back corner and pushes it open for me to walk out first. Just like that we are absorbed into the quiet of outside in the back of the building.

On a regular day or night it is just a yard of grass, but tonight there was a mess of cars parked all the way back to the fence. Melanie's Audi included and untouched.

A. ERIN WALKER

The cool air of the night hits my exposed legs and sends a shiver up my spine, but it feels so good compared to the mugginess inside the hall.

We walk over to one of the bench's lined up against the building, which is probably where employees come for lunch and smoke breaks judging by the cigarette buds scattered all over the ground.

"I said I'll make sure you get a signed copy... Nothing major." Dylan laughs and I can see the reflection of the full moon in the ball of his eyes.

I cross my legs to get comfortable on the hard bench and set my phone down beside me. He reaches into his pocket. I look up towards the nighttime sky.

The moon almost appears to be within arms reach, its white fullness contrasting against the dark sky. It appears larger and the small stars surrounding it shine as much as they can above the lights of the city.

"It's such a beautiful night." I say, studying the gray spots on the moon's surface.

"It really is," his hand comes out of the pocket holding a lighter and he pulls a blunt out of his other pocket before pausing. "I'm sorry, do you mind?"

I shake my head letting him continue and watch as he places the blunt between his lips and flicks the lighter against it.

The fire burns a bright orange with every puff that he takes and smoke escapes from his mouth as he lights up the drug. He inhales and holds it in, allowing the THC to circulate through his lungs as his eyes glance back to me and his arm extends the blunt in my direction.

"No, thanks." I say.

He pulls it back to him, exhaling the smoke up and into the sky. "It's been a long day," He grins.

"I bet." I return a toothless smile and look down at the polluted grass.

I can feel him staring at me. I try to give my best displays of effortless beauty, looking back toward the sky as I pretend that I cannot feel him watching my every move.

Several clicks can be heard from the shutter of his camera, so I spin my head back towards him as he is replacing the tool onto his lap. The smile still planted on his face.

"You're supposed to be taking pictures of Jay, not me," I laugh. "Let me see how they look," I reach for the camera but he leans out the way.

"I have more than enough footage of Jay, trust me… and no, you can't see. Just know they're perfect."

"I am definitely not perfect." I downplay his compliment as I glance away, careful not to blush.

"I didn't say you were. I was talking about the pictures. They're perfect. Because I took them." He bursts into laughter as I smack his leg playfully.

Silence falls upon us. The only noises heard are coming from the muffled sounds of music inside of the building and the occasional car passing by.

Dylan takes another hit of his blunt. Inhale. Hold. Exhale to the sky.

"So, what's your story, Dylan?" I break our silence, no longer able to contain my curiosity.

"My story?" His eyes are low and still shining under the moonlight as he turns to look at me.

"Yes, your story. Are you from here?"

He leans back against the wall of the building. "Nope, I'm from Chicago. I moved out here about a year ago to further my photography career."

My interest increases, "It wasn't going too well back home?" I shift to face more in his direction, placing a hand on the bench to hold up the weight of my body.

"Ehh... It was going. Things were just a little tough. My mom tried her best but taking care of three boys can take a toll, especially when you're forced to do it alone. And the death of my little sister a few years ago... That really hurt us," Dylan's eyes fall empty as I find him staring into space. I fix my lips to give my condolences but he goes on before I can. "I always offered to get a job but she didn't want me to lose focus on school and my art," Life returns to his eyes and his voice warms, "She is the sweetest woman I'll ever know."

"I'm sorry about your sister."

"Yeah..."

Silence.

"Did you go to school at all?" I break the silence again.

"Yep. The Art Institute of Chicago. It was pretty expensive but I took out loans to pay for it so my mom didn't have to worry much."

"So, you must be pretty decent with that camera," I joke.

"Ha! This camera is my everything. I'm way more than decent, young Tamryn."

He goes on to explain how the idea of moving to California was born after being presented with an opportunity about two years ago. One of the professors at his school accepted a job offer with a motion picture company to be their Director of Photography. He would have an important role in arranging the perfect images to be displayed in films that he was put in charge of, as well as hiring the right photographers to assist him. The professor was somewhat of a mentor to Dylan, so when he accepted the offer he extended one of his own to him. A few months after the professor moved out here and got settled, Dylan followed him and was prepared to work on whatever set that he was called for.

This connection enabled Dylan to network at many events thrown by the company, meeting more and more clientele as he spoke with people and shared his work. Eventually he started getting booked for photo shoots from graduation celebrations to weddings. He also became a personal photographer for up and coming musical artists such as Jay and Wide Awake that were trying to perfect their images in the industry.

The calls still come in from the professor but they're irregular. Yet, Dylan has built his brand and reputation well enough over this past year of being in the city that he is able to make a living with or without the professor's assignments.

"I wire money to my mom every month and I always make sure that I make it home for every birthday and holiday. I just want to do my best for her, honestly."

Inhale. Hold. Exhale to the sky.

"That is beyond respectable, Dylan. Taking care of your mom as soon as you got the chance. That's how it should be." I admire him for choosing to take a huge step by moving away from his family to follow his dreams and keeping them as his number one priority. Now that his dream has become his profession, he is able to help his mother in ways that may have taken much longer, if they were possible at all, to accomplish if he would have stayed at home.

Dylan nods his head as he puts out the blunt, rubbing it into the bench. "Yeah, so now that you know my story... It's your turn to share."

I take a brief moment to configure the proper words to explain my story, regarding the fact that I came out here to discover exactly what that is. I take a deep breath and glance over to find him watching me and waiting patiently.

"I started having these dreams. They would make me feel as though I'm... Trapped... Suffocating. At the time, I was in school studying a major I cared nothing about, just for the possibility to end up in a job I might not even like. I was surrounded by people who were either okay with this outcome and justifying it by saying that's just how life goes, or people who were okay with doing absolutely nothing special. Just complaining about their situation while they watched life pass by. I did not want to end up in either of those categories. I could not accept that the one life intended for me is meant to be wasted, slaving my life away having nothing to look forward to but the occasional vacation day. Or trying to be a local celebrity amongst a group of clones that would rather watch you struggle with them than support you. Especially when there are people in the world actually doing what they love to do... Like you. I just wanted to take a risk and see where it landed me. Stop wasting my energy and channel it to just going out and finding what I'm looking for. Myself. A passion. I don't know..." My voice trails off as I start to lose the words.

Dylan asks me to tell him about the dream.

So, I give him a rundown of the grueling nightmare that used to wake me up in the middle of the night with beads of sweat on my forehead and the fear of dying unhappy in my heart.

Silence.

Maybe I should not have told him.

"Do you still have the nightmare?" Dylan asks, leaning forward and appearing to be staring at nothing in particular.

I cannot even read the blank expression on his face for any clues of what he may be thinking. "Actually, no. I have not had it in a while."

Back to silence.

I hope he does not find me childish. Here I am whining about a nightmare that I had a few times like a little girl. I can only imagine that he must be trying to conjure the correct pattern of words to politely let me know that I need to grow up.

"I feel as though," Dylan finally begins to speak, his voice filled with a serious concentration like he was interpreting a code to a safe that held the cure for cancer. "That glass box that you were stuck in was a closed mindset. One preventing you from experiencing everything that life has to offer due to being surrounded by and seeing so many people who are perfectly fine with that, such as the people who were dancing and having fun around you. Yet, you have no desire to be like them. You have something deep inside of you that is pushing you to be great, and it's too strong for you to ignore. When you left your city and took this risk to create yourself and discover your calling, you escaped the limit that was placed on yourself and your life. Maybe that's why you haven't had the nightmare since. That's what I think." He turns his head back towards me and our eyes meet for what feels like an eternity.

The words he just uttered flowed so naturally, with no problem. He sat there and practically decoded my life in less than a minute with no sweat off his back.

Didn't I say the artists always seem to understand me the most?

Dylan inches his body closer toward me on the bench and I look forward, breaking the intimacy of our eye contact.

His leg is touching mine. He brings his hand up to my face, using two fingers to slightly turn it back toward him.

An inch away. Eye to eye. Nose to nose. Lips to lips.

He tilts his head and slowly moves in for the kill, the smell of marijuana overpowering the mint on his breath. Our lips touch gently, and the softness of his sends that electric shock throughout my body all over again.

But before I can muster up any thought of whether or not I wanted this to go on, I pull back and turn my head. The moment is abruptly ended.

I'm just not ready for this.

"Hey," Dylan's voice is tender as he turns my face back toward his. He is flashing the sweetest smile and his thick eyebrows are furrowed with concern. "I don't want anything you're not ready for. You're the coolest female that I've met in a long time. I guess I just got ahead of myself and I apologize."

"You don't have to apologize, seriously. I'm sorry, I just-,"

"Trust me, Tamryn, I get it," His eyes continue to hold mine captive and refuse to loosen their grip. "But, if it's no problem we have to… HAVE to… agree to be friends. I won't let you deny me that." He laughs, bringing me to laughter too.

"We can definitely be friends. Thank you for being so understanding."

My sweet new friend Dylan, the photographer.

I look down as my phone vibrates from its position on the bench, the screen displaying "Mel" with a picture of us together that I assigned as her caller ID. "Hey," I put the phone to my ear as I answer the call.

Melanie's background is loud with the voices of people but no music. "Where the hell are you!?" She yells. I cannot tell if she is trying to be heard over all the noise or if she is angry.

I stand up, starting to see people come around the building to the yard of cars. The show must be over. "I'm sitting with Dylan behind the building, where are you?"

"Meet me at my car." She hangs up.

Dylan stands, all 6'2" of his body towering over me and routinely moves his camera out the way as he reaches in for a hug. "I'm gonna head back inside to find Jay so he doesn't think I screwed him on the visuals," He pulls me into him and I try not to melt as the side of my face meets his chest. "Where's your cousin?"

"She should be heading back here now. I'm going to meet her at the car."

"Want me to walk with you?"

I look to the back of the lot where Melanie's sports car rests. The lights flicker as a hastily walking Melanie hits the button to unlock the doors as she approaches it.

Something must have happened during the concert, because even from a distance her demeanor appears to be bothered. I hope it wasn't those guys from the table she was at.

I look up to Dylan, "No, it's okay. She's over there already. Thanks again." I take a deep breath of his scent as I squeeze my arms around him in our embrace and his strong arm squeezes me back hard enough to make up for his other hand holding the camera.

He pulls out his phone and places the device into my hand for me to save my number.

I dial the digits. Enter my name. *Save.*

He promises to text me in a few minutes so that I can have his number as well.

Walking through the lot of cars to get back to Melanie's car has become an obstacle course as I *zigzag* through the crowd of drunken concert-goers. It is funny to think that just a few moments ago this entire area was dead silent. Now it is taken over with chit-chat and random sounds of the excessive amount of people who have abandoned the inside of the concert hall.

I glance over my shoulder for a brief moment as people pass through my view to find Dylan still standing where I left him. He is watching to make sure that I arrive at Melanie's car safely.

I smile. My whole insides are smiling.

I may have ruined a picture-perfect moment with Dylan by pulling away from his kiss, but it has resulted in our starting a beautiful friendship. A friendship that has exceptional potential to be more. But, not by rushing or forcing it.

When I have said that I am not in this city with a primary objective of dating or finding the love of my life, I meant it. But, I am at the will of the universe, so whatever is meant to be will be.

Whatever is meant for me will always be for me. And whatever is not will not.

Pulling open the passenger-side door and sliding into the car, I see Melanie is already fastening her seatbelt.

I follow suit as her foot presses on the brake pedal while her finger presses on the glowing "Push to Start" button located by the steering wheel.

The engine awakes and the car is cut on, causing Melanie's blue headlights to glow as well as the blue lights of all the various gadgets on the dashboard.

"I loved the show, Mel. You were right... Jay is an awesome singer."

The lot appears just as difficult to get out of as it was to get into with all the cars backed up and waiting to exit. We may be sitting here for a while.

"Really? You weren't even inside to enjoy it." Melanie's voice is dry and her eyes are on her phone.

Hmm.

As much as I want to know what is going on inside of my cousin's mind, I know that she has never been the greatest at expressing her feelings. As long as I am not the issue I already know that she will let me in when she is ready to let me in.

So, I ignore the tone in her voice, sit back and stare out my window in an attempt to dodge her negative vibrations.

"Why didn't you text me when you found Dylan?" Melanie asks, her question bringing my attention back toward her to find her eyes trying to cut me into tiny little pieces.

I guess I am the issue.

"Oh... I must have forgotten. It's not that big a deal."

"You left the building, Tam. I was searching high and low for you when the show ended and you were out here with him the entire time. What if something would have happened? I would have been trying to find you like a dumb shit looking in the wrong place."

Whoa.

There are two or three accounts that can be immediately recalled of Melanie and I ever arguing and she wants to add something as insignificant as this to the list? Because I came outside with a guy? When that bar stool tipped forward, I must have really fell and landed back in eighth grade.

I stare forward through the windshield and wish that these cars would move faster to bring this conversation to an end as soon as possible. "If you were so worried why didn't you call or text me when you realized I hadn't texted you yet?"

"Because you're grown as hell. I figured you found him and were sitting somewhere *inside* of the building enjoying the show. You just met him earlier, what if he knocked your little ass out once he got you out that backdoor? You must want to end up in somebody's trunk. One-way trip to human trafficking?"

I giggle at her extreme scenario. "Okay, you're overreacting."

Her voice gets louder to prove that my laughter is not fit for this discussion. "I'm not overreacting I am thinking the way an adult should think, which is realistically. You're over there in dreamland believing everybody is trustworthy or some shit. You don't know that guy! You're a smart young woman, you should act like it sometimes," She rolls her eyes away from me accompanied with a deep sigh. "Look... Next time... Please, just shoot me a text, Tam. To let me know that you are not where I may be thinking you are. That is all."

I nod my head.

Sheesh. All of this over a text message.

I can understand her being worried when she discovered that I was not inside of the building anymore but at the same time it is not like I completely left the premises.

We sit in silence for a moment, the cars finally moving fast enough for Melanie to pull up into the line and begin rolling us out the lot of *the Crawlspace*.

She presses the volume button that is conveniently located on her steering wheel to turn up the radio, filling the car with Tupac's "Gangsta Party".

My phone vibrates in my lap with a text message from a phone number starting with a "213" area code: *It's Dylan, lock me in. Get home safely.*

My mind goes back to the feeling of the fluttering butterflies within my stomach that I experienced prior to getting into the car with Melanie. I had a very nice night until now, but I won't let myself dwell on her words.

The few times that we have ever had disagreements never caused ill feelings that lasted more than a day. Melanie and I will always wield the strength of our sisterly relationship for the good of each other, not to hold on to grudges.

Everything will be back to normal tomorrow.

I respond back to Dylan and save his number. Now I am just looking forward to getting back to the apartment, taking a long shower, grabbing my ID and chapstick out of Melanie's clutch (purposely leaving the ten-dollar bill), and passing out on the futon.

Seven.

Cleveland, 2000

Three years have come and gone since the passing of Mark Williams.

Things have gotten tougher just as Melanie anticipated. Her Aunt Shannon had always worked third shift at the hospital, but now she had been picking up any available first and second shifts in order to take care of her niece.

Additionally, Melanie was now at the growing and confusing age of eleven, where her life began to change forever as she is abruptly introduced to puberty. Thrown into a whirlwind of physical and emotional bewilderment.

Welcome to womanhood.

Melanie was reluctant to share the happenings of her body with Shannon. She was nervous that everything going on were signs of some serious issues that she did not want to burden her Aunt with.

But Shannon took notice.

They may not have shared a relationship that was as close as Melanie would have liked, but her aunt was still her aunt as well as a fellow woman. So, no words needed to be exchanged in order for Shannon to see the growing pains that were attempting to swallow her niece whole.

Shannon was sure to explain the purpose and technicalities of menstrual cycles as well as female health in general. She also explained the discipline required to handle the new swarm of hormones that Melanie was experiencing.

They took a field trip to the nearest drug store and Melanie was shown the vast array of options she had to choose from when it comes to pads and tampons.

The regulars, the supers, the pearls, the heavies, the ultrathins.

But before her little head could spin from all of the differences, Shannon tossed the most basic padding selection into Melanie's basket to start her off and kept things as simple as possible.

It was also time for bra shopping, during which Shannon waited patiently as a sales associate measured

Melanie and explained the important purpose of her training bra in protecting her new *ta-ta*'s.

All of this assistance and preparation made Melanie feel grateful as she was forced to deal with the changes. But she could not shake the notion that, even though she could not help it, everything was just stressing out her aunt even more. Because of the extra shopping trips, Shannon lost a couple hours of sleep that she is usually able to have before heading into work at night. Melanie knew how important it was that Aunt Shannon got her rest for those long nights at the hospital. And even though Uncle Mark was no longer present for Melanie to overhear their conversations, she couldn't help but to believe that her aunt's thoughts were filled with frustration.

But what could she do?

It may have been divine intervention when Shannon came across Travis Rene a couple weeks later at the grocery store.

Travis was a few years younger than Shannon in his early thirties. But he had maturity and charm so intense that she could not help but to fall in love with him almost as quickly as he fell in love with her.

Travis seemed to deliver a burst of sunshine and happiness to, not only Shannon, but Melanie as well. Melanie valued Travis for being so abundantly nice to her that his characteristics began to overflow onto her Aunt Shannon and made her loosen up too.

That man brought smiles to Shannon's face that Melanie thought had been deactivated forever. She knew he could do nothing but make their lives easier just by being around.

And he did that plus much more.

One thing that Melanie loved about Travis was that he did and said everything sincerely.

He told the both of them everything and never tried to put on a front. He was a gentleman that dressed well and paid for groceries before carrying them into Shannon's house in his sleek button-down shirts and dress-pants. He opened up about his past when he wasn't the best version of himself that he could have been. He admitted to making mistakes and committing acts that he wasn't proud of growing up in the inner city, but that was what ultimately led him to become the successful man that he had become today.

Travis shared the significance of when he changed his last name to Rene, translating to *reborn* in

Latin and serving as a constant reminder of the new life he had created for himself.

A successful life that could have been ended prematurely if he would have continued down his initial path of destruction.

But now, he was the owner of several car dealerships around the city, working hard for every dollar that he had earned. And he had certainly earned a great deal of dollars.

Travis never showed up empty-handed when he stopped by, always carrying gifts for his woman as well as Melanie. He even planned weekend getaways with Shannon at least once a month, which Melanie may not be invited to, but she got to spend those weekends at her Aunt Patricia's house with a cute and quiet Tamryn who had just started the first grade. They always woke up early and helped Aunt Patricia fix their favorite blueberry pancakes, which she always let Melanie flip to perfection while Tamryn looked up at her big cousin and smiled, her little eyes filled with adoration.

Travis was also a mentor to young boys all around the city of Cleveland. He made sure that he could be a positive male-figure for them to depend on, while reassuring them that a life in the streets was not a life for them to live. And a couple of months into Travis and Shannon's relationship, he introduced the ladies to the most important young boy in his life, his fifteen year old son, TJ.

TJ and Melanie instantly clicked.

He became the brother that she never had and they were always able to confide in one another about the struggles of friendships and growing up, in general.

They even shared something more special in common than the secrets and stories of their adolescence, TJ also being deprived of a relationship with his mother. She left TJ and Travis when he was about five years old for a reason that Travis would not explain any more to his son than that she was tired of dealing with the ways of the man that he was back then. They were never married, so besides leaving the little boy that she had loved and raised for five years of her life, disappearing was just a matter of leaving and taping a note to their apartment door.

Travis had no choice, upon finding that note in an attempt to return TJ to his mother after one of their short visitations, but to start growing up and becoming a real man that could take care of his son. Was an unfortunate tale of a young boy who lost his mother's love due to her insensitivity, which was why Melanie could relate to him so well. She may have never experienced love from her mother for it to truly be lost, but it was always missed.

And the love from Shannon that never seemed genuine was now being made up for in the love Melanie was beginning to feel from TJ. As well as Melanie witnessing the love that Travis showered Shannon with that was powerful enough to fill an entire room. Their relationship had to be strong enough to reduce the distance between Shannon and Melanie's relationship by filling Shannon with so much love and care that she would let go of the resentment she held towards her little sister.

At least this was what Melanie hoped for.

And it seemed that outcome would attain a greater possibility when Travis suggested, nine months into their relationship, that they all take a weekend trip to Myrtle Beach. Melanie was nothing less than elated as she watched Travis pull out his phone to contact his travel agent. She had never even been outside of the state of Ohio and the thought of experiencing an actual family vacation filled her with so much joy she could have popped like a balloon.

It seemed as though the seven days between the arrangements being made and the morning of their departure went by slow enough to be mistaken for a month. Travis and TJ arrived at Shannon's house at the crack of dawn on that Thursday morning, packed Travis' truck with their bags, and they hit the road to South Carolina.

Melanie slept the first few hours of the ten-hour long drive then kept herself awake the rest of the ride. She stared out the window as they drove through West Virginia, Virginia, North Carolina, and indulged in the views of finally reaching the shores of Myrtle Beach.

She was forced to hold back tears of exhilaration as her watering eyes captured the sight of the endless Atlantic Ocean from the balcony of their condominium.

Upon the group's arrival that evening, they enjoyed dinner at a small seafood restaurant that was just a short walk away from their temporary abode. Then a good amount of the rest of the weekend was spent shopping, Travis swiping his credit card for numerous outfits and souvenirs for everybody.

The rest of the time was spent at the beach.

TJ and Melanie would play around in the water and joined in to play volleyball at neighboring hotels harboring kids in their age range. Travis and Shannon would lay out and fall asleep under the sun on their beach chair, occasionally getting up to play in the water as if they were fifteen years younger.

Then Saturday evening, just before it was time for the sun to lower in the sky and hide behind the horizon of the ocean, Travis spotted the jet-ski rentals and decided to turn the final hours of their vacation up a notch.

"I am not getting on that thing," Shannon said with her arms folded across her chest and an eyebrow raised as she stood at the stand with Melanie and TJ, watching Travis pay for two jet-skis. Shannon always had a thick figure just like her two sisters, and her curves were emphasized by the baby blue one-piece swimsuit she decided to wear that day.

"Babe, what? I thought you were my ride-or-die?" Travis raised an eyebrow back to his girlfriend that sent Melanie and TJ into a parade of giggles.

"Whatever, I'm going to grab a chair and lay my ass down. You folks are crazy, I've seen how fast those things go."

Travis called after her but she was already in hot pursuit to one empty chair that she quickly spotted out of a million occupied ones.

Since it was assumed that Travis would be driving one of the aquatic vehicles and TJ would be driving the other, Melanie was left with the decision of which one she wanted to ride on the back of. She watched as TJ got situated on his jet-ski and goofily flexed his newly acquired muscles that he had been working hard for in daily basketball practices to his father. Travis rolled his eyes with an accompanying smirk at his son and Melanie felt the ankle-deep waters of the shore slip between her toes as she headed in his direction.

Travis helped her climb onto the back of his ride and warned her to hold on tight.

Melanie did not need to be told twice as she wrapped her arms around his torso with all of her might, growing anxious as she listened to the engine growl like a Rottweiler ready to attack. Travis started out driving slowly and Melanie laughed as she looked over his shoulder at the sight of TJ already zooming across the water like he had no sense.

They made their way out to a wider range of the allotted riding space and before Melanie could prepare herself, he pressed all the way on the throttle throwing them into full-speed. She dug her cheek into Travis' sun-kissed, chocolate-toned back and strengthened her grip on his stomach as water splashed into her face with every bump their jet-ski took against the waves of the ocean. She regretted the decision of participating in this activity with the guys every time their ride hit a wave and her small frame bounced up into the air.

"Woo hoo! Yeah!" Travis yelled out as they raced across the water and his adrenaline rush began to kick his testosterone levels into high gear.

Melanie was holding on for her life, knowing if she loosened her grip even a little bit she just might be thrown into the ocean to swim with the fishes.

She heard Travis yell out, "What's up, son!?" and fought the splashing water hitting her face long enough to peek her head up and see their crossing paths with TJ.

The fifteen year-old was coming from the opposite direction hollering, "Yeahhhhh!", bringing Melanie back to a sense of enjoyment in the water sport.

As they darted past him she threw an arm up to wave and TJ smiled big, revealing the gap between his two front teeth that the young girls at his school found so adorable.

While Melanie's hand was still in the air, Travis cut the handle of the jet-ski. A sharp turn was initiated that aggressively bounced the vehicle against the waves to turn it in the opposite direction and chase after TJ. The arm that Melanie still had wrapped around Travis lost it's grip, flinging her into the ocean before she could even blink.

Melanie kept her eyes closed tightly as she felt herself floating beneath the water, and before she could realize she hadn't held her breath the life jacket strapped around her body sprung her up and above the surface.

She shook her head, sending the two shoulder length cornrows of her hair into a frenzy and wiped the water from her face. Then she open her eyes to the sight of TJ pulling up beside her with his arm extended and Travis not too far behind.

"My dad tossed you from his ride, huh?" TJ helped her onto the back of his jet-ski, careful to maintain his balance while laughing.

"I am so sorry, sweetheart! I should have been paying more attention. I told you to hold on, though!" Travis gave an unsuccessful attempt at hiding his laughter, his dark brown skin developing a slightly red tone as a smile spread across his face.

Melanie couldn't help but to laugh at herself when she imagined the sight of her body being flung from Travis' jet-ski like a rag doll and she held on to TJ with a tight grip as he drove back to the docks.

A clapping and laughing Shannon was there waiting for them.

They all returned to the condo just after the sunset. Travis and Shannon freshened up to hurry right back out of the door for a romantic night on the town. It was the last night of their vacation and Travis wanted to make sure that he and his lady spent some quality time together.

No kids allowed.

When they left, Melanie was sitting on the pull-out bed of the sofa watching a documentary on television about whales and TJ was in the bathroom getting out of the shower. Their condo had a small kitchenette, one master bedroom for the adults equipped with an en-suite, a pullout sofa bed in the living room that Melanie claimed upon their arrival, a regular couch that belonged to TJ for the weekend, and another bathroom located on the other side of the living room that TJ just walked out of wearing a wife beater, fresh pair of cargo shorts, and his favorite pair of Air Jordan sneakers.

"Going somewhere?" Melanie asked when she noticed his outfit change and a hint of his dad's cologne that he sprayed.

"The guys we played volleyball with earlier said I should come have a beer with them tonight," TJ brushed his light brown wavy hair.

Melanie rolled her eyes and looked back to the TV trying not to be annoyed about not being invited. And avoiding the idea of being petty and telling on him.

The boys that they were playing volleyball with were only around TJ's age, but they are staying with older family members that are legal and seemed uncaring enough to let the minors indulge in a beer or two.

TJ asked Melanie to cover for him in case Shannon and his dad returned before he did and she agreed, regardless of her sour feelings towards not being invited.

He picked up the extra key to the condo off of the counter in the kitchenette and placed it in his pocket with his wallet and small cellphone, then headed out of the door. Melanie was left alone at the drop of a dime.

The sudden loneliness was close to upsetting her on this final night of their "family vacation" until memories of the last few days ran through her mind like a movie. The view of the whales on the television had been replaced and a smile was back onto her face. She just had the best weekend that she had probably ever had in her life and nothing, including this unexpected moment of solitude, could ruin that for her.

Travis and TJ had become people whom she could genuinely trust and her aunt was appearing to be happier than she had been in a while. The trip had proven to Melanie that the possibilities of life were endless, just like the dark ocean shining under the night stars that she could see just by turning her head and looking out of the sliding doors of the balcony.

Melanie returned from her thoughts and went into the bathroom to shower and get ready to call it a night. She threw on her pajamas and cut out the light in the living room, then slid into her sofa bed and curled up under the covers. Her eyes stared out at the ocean and the night sky until her beautiful realities turn into sweet dreams.

An unknown amount of time passed and she was awakened by the swipe of a key and a *click* as the door was opened. There is only one set of footsteps so she knew it was TJ, and she smiled to herself when she heard him bump into the kitchen counter.

His footsteps went into the bathroom for a brief moment then he returned to the living room. Melanie was sure to maintain the same position facing the balcony door to keep the appearance of still being asleep.

She feels the bed depress slightly as he gently climbs in beside her and her eyes widen. She tries to figure out what he is doing getting into her bed when his location for sleeping has been the other couch this entire weekend.

She stays frozen in place as TJ scooted in closer to her and wrapped his arm around her waist, then moved his hand from her stomach down to the side of her leg.

Melanie springs her body to sit up as fast as a Jack jumping out of the box, embarrassed that his touches sent a pleasurable thrill throughout her body. "What are you doing?" She looked down at TJ, whose head is still lying on the pillow and light brown eyes staring at her.

He let out a small laugh. "I don't even know." And he sat up to meet Melanie with a smile, combatting the nervousness written all over her face.

Melanie was rushed with a tsunami of mixed emotions from scared to allured to ashamed. "You need to get out of my bed, TJ. How many beers did you have?"

The smile on his face has yet to subside as he blinks slowly and crawls out of her bed. He tugged the top cover off with him and falls onto the other couch.

Melanie clenched the bed sheet she was left with as she watched TJ obey her request and simultaneously ignored her question. She laid back down, this time facing in his direction with her eyes glued to the back of his head. She listened as his breathing became snores, and only then did she take her eyes off him.

Looking back to the television, she tried to tame her mind that was running as wild as the giraffes being followed in the current documentary on the screen.

Trying to decipher what just occurred was nearly impossible, but she refused to allow her eyes to close until Travis and her Aunt Shannon came tip-toeing through the door.

Eight.

Los Angeles, Present Day

Hints of a brightening sky were just beginning to show when I reached the rooftop.

The pink blanket I had been sleeping under every night since I arrived is wrapped around my shoulders as I plant myself down on the same couch Melanie and I sat upon the other night.

The temperature was a little lower during this time of the morning, so I threw on a hoodie and a cozy pair of leggings. But my feet were revealed to the brisk air from failing to put on socks before I slipped on my Nike sandals, so I kicked off the footwear and swung my feet up and underneath my bottom to warm my toes.

The sounds of cars passing by filled my ears more than I was expecting with it being just a little after six in the morning. Then I remembered I am no longer in the quiet suburb that I grew up in on the outskirts of

Cleveland. One could almost mistake my old neighborhood for a ghost town at this time. There would be just one or two stragglers out and ready to conquer the day before the sun rose. But now I am surrounded by the unfamiliar and constant hustle and bustle of Los Angeles.

I guess this is one of those cities that never sleeps.

The cars passing by could be occupied by dreamchasers that refuse to rest until they reach their achievements. Maybe they left the comfort of their hometowns to make it in the big city, like me. Or perhaps they were raised here and are taking advantage of the opportunities right in their backyard. Maybe they are driving home from a late-night rendezvous this Friday morning after quenching their thirsty Thursdays. They might still have on their clothes from last night as they head back to the comfort of their own beds.

Drives of shame.

Trying to guess the lifestyles of the mysterious beings is enticing, especially with them possessing not one bit of knowledge of my existence five stories above them.

My observant nature always keeps my wheels turning, but in this moment I want nothing more than to clear my head and allow myself to just sit and take in all of the unfamiliarities. All of my senses are engaged as I unwind and open up to my environment; the blending of colors across the sky as the sun pushes itself above the landscape of buildings in my view, the sounds of the vehicles as they make their way passed the apartment building way below myself on the ground, and the occasional soft breeze brushing my wild curls against the side of my face. As I am drifting into the most peaceful and conscious moment of the week thus far, the first thing that manages to pop into my mind is the thought of my parents.

I reach into the pocket of my hoodie to pull out my phone and dial my mother's number. The voices of the people who love me the most would be the cherry on top of my sweet morning.

"Hello, Tamryn!" My mom answers the phone after just one ring and I can hear her smile beaming through her voice. "I was just thinking about you. You're on speaker phone, your dad is right here with me!"

AWAY

"Hey, baby!" My dad's deep voice chimes in to confirm his presence and I am overwhelmed with joy in feeling their love through the phone.

"Hey mommy, hey daddy! What are you guys up to?"

"We just got in the car. Your dad has to take me to work this morning because my car is in the shop. What are you doing, baby?"

I rest my head against the back of the couch and close my eyes, imagining that I am in the backseat of my father's navy blue Chrysler 300 as he drives with one hand on the wheel and the other hand's fingers interlocked with my mother's. His bald head shining as the sun unleashes its rays through the sunroof and my mom's long, black curly mane blowing in the wind as she stares out of the open passenger-side window.

I can almost smell his "Black Ice" car freshener.

"I'm just watching the sunrise on the rooftop. I miss you guys."

"Watching the sunrise on the rooftop!?" My dad's voice thunders in the background. "Tam, we should have left you here and moved to Los Angeles our damn selves! There was a snowstorm last night and it's about negative four degrees right now!" I giggle at the thought of my father's thick eyebrows furrowed in a fake jealous rage as he maneuvers the car through the remains of a blizzard that coated the city the night before.

My fantasy of sitting in the backseat of my father's car as we cruise in the sunshine has been bombarded with the realistic thought of wearing my big, purple winter jacket, rubbing my gloves together to warm up my hands. My dad's shining bald head hiding beneath his favorite Ohio State beanie as my mother's hand still rests in his, cold and patiently waiting for the car to warm up.

I open my eyes to bring the scene to an end and my body shivers. Memories of the brutal winters of Ohio make this "cool" morning air of California feel like a tickle.

"I hope you guys are all bundled up."

"Of course, Tam. So, how are you? I love the pictures you sent me from the beach. Send me some pictures of any celebrities you see too. Did you do anything fun last night?" My mom's voice is just dripping with interest in how my move has been so far. This phone call is way overdue since I have only been texting and sending her pictures since I got here, but I had to make sure I was comfortably settled in so that our first real conversation since my departure was not swamped with complaints.

The last thing I would want to do is drop out of school and leave the state just to whine to them about my decision. My parents have always been kind and understanding, but they don't hesitate to curse me out when it is deemed necessary.

"I'm fine. Good, I took them just for you. And okay, I will," I take a breath of fresh air as I watch the darkest parts of the sky slowly blend with the light of the rising sun and become light blue. "We went to a concert for one of Melanie's friends. He's an awesome singer so it was a nice show."

"Her boyfriend?"

Here goes her handy dandy fishing rod for the information she has been waiting for.

She is preparing to get the answers about my dating life, first by introducing the topic with a question regarding Melanie's. I am all too familiar with the way my mother's curiosity operates and the hook has just been tied onto her fishing line.

"No, mom, just her friend."

"Oh okay. Have you seen any cute guys out there?" The bait has been applied to the hook.

"I've seen a few."

"Hmm. Any of special interest?" The line has been casted into the sea, and she is now awaiting to hear about my fresh catch.

"Kind of." I express my interest in Dylan and tell her about the great time we shared together last night, being sure to leave out our small kiss because some things are better left unsaid. Especially with a father listening in that is always more than ready to "*protect his precious baby girl from the sex-craving men of the world and their dirty intentions, because none of them are innocent and they all want to steal your goodie bag*".

His words.

"Dylan sounds nice, Tam." My mom's voice is filled with delight. "That sounds like a lovely evening."

"It was," I begin. "At least until Melanie freaked out on me."

"She did what?" My mom and dad question my last words in unison, as if they are prepared to send their car in the direction of Cleveland-Hopkins Airport and hop on the next plane to southern California.

"She just got mad at me for not telling her that I was in the back of the building with Dylan. She said I could have gotten sold into human trafficking and should stop trusting people in *dreamland* or something like that. I still don't understand why she was so upset but whatever." My eyes roll at the memory of Melanie's words crashing against my ears in all of their dramatic glory. I hate that I've brought the situation back into my thoughts.

"Well," My dad starts, "I can agree with Mel in saying that you shouldn't trust people so easily because you really should not and I would prefer that you did not. But, you are also a very smart young woman and she should not have gotten that upset with you."

"But, I'm happy that she did, Tam," My mom interjects, "That shows that she really cares about your well-being! I will be able to sleep a little better tonight knowing that Mel is looking out for you and willing to share her concerns when she is worried."

My mother's perspective was not what I expected and wanted to hear, but then again, my parents never tell me what I want to hear. They have these special powers where they are able to shine light on situations with their insight, allowing me to recollect things from a different point of view.

My mother's soft words hit me as if someone threw a bucket of flowers in my face.

Melanie cares about me. People may express caring in many different ways, but now that I have removed my veil of selfishness I can see that I probably would have reacted the same way if I was worried about her.

Lesson learned.

My parents and I exchanged *I love you*'s and I made a new commitment to start calling a lot more often. I almost wanted to cry as we hung up, but I fought the urge for sadness with feelings of gratitude.

Gratitude to my family. Gratitude to my journey. Gratitude to this beautiful ass rooftop view.

I slip my feet back into my sandals and keep thinking of how Patricia and James are my greatest gifts from God. That God that has allowed me to watch the sun rise into the sky and be present during the birth of this brand new day and its numerous opportunities. I carry myself back down to the fourth floor, glowing with rejuvenation as I return to the loft.

"For the love of money…"

I had fallen back asleep on the sectional in the living area, but I was now waking up to the booming bass of a song all-too familiar to me.

As all my senses awakened, my ears began to pick up the voices of hip hop legends and Cleveland natives, Bone Thugs-N-Harmony. Their classic tune of one of my favorite singles was blasting through the wireless speakers that occupied three corners of the room, so I forced my eyes open and glanced over the pink bed sheet to find Melanie dancing and staring at me about two feet away from the couch.

She is wearing a black crop top, exposing her flat tummy and pierced belly-button with black leggings. Her black bob haircut sways from side-to-side as she moves her body to the beat and keeps her brown eyes locked on me in the creepiest way possible. "Heyyyyyy, young Tam! What do you know about this song, with your young butt?" She yells over the beat and I cannot help but to laugh, remembering the first time I ever listened to the rap group when she left their "Creepin' On Ah Come Up" CD at my house and accused me of lying when I told her I lost it.

Of course I was lying. She knew me too well, being fully aware that I knew exactly where it was and never wanted to return it. And she still knows me too well, using this song to stir up memories of our childhood and bury any awkwardness that resulted from last night's situation.

All I can think about now is the sight before me of my goofy, loud, overbearing, and unpredictable big cousin challenging me with her moves to get up and join her.

I peel myself off the couch to match her dances with some of my own, one hand in the air as I nod my head and grind my hips to the beat. "I know more than you think!"

We dance and rap the popular lyrics to the song, letting our hometown roots and style be the elixir to heal the small scratches and scrapes left on our relationship in last night's argument.

Even if my parents had not eased my thoughts on what happened, this would have been enough to get me over it.

Melanie is the only person I have ever been close enough to where our disagreements are dead and buried so quickly. If the same issue would have occurred between myself and a regular friend of mine, I probably would have never spoken to that friend again.

"Okay, okay, okay... So I have a huge surprise for you!" Melanie hits the volume button on the speakers' remote control several times to tone down the music and our dance party.

"More jewelry from Tiffany's?"

"You wish," Melanie laughs. "Ronald is having a HUGE birthday bash at one of his clubs tonight and SHE Inc. will be one of the guest hostess groups! Your first night as a party rep is TONIGHT!" She grabs my arms and jumps up and down, forcing excitement to have a hostile takeover inside my body and blood rushing to my head in nervousness.

Wait.

"Tonight!? What the... I just washed my hair in the shower last night, now I have to wash it again and straighten it! What am I going to wear? Why are you telling me about this so late?" I am blowing around in a tornado of uncertainty, the natural disaster being created by my brain in less than three seconds.

A new record for me.

If tonight is my first night hanging with the big dogs, I need to get my puppy behind in gear!

"Whoa, there. Relax," Melanie keeps her hands on my arms and gives a squeeze of encouragement. "We are all wearing white dresses that were delivered to the boutique about two hours ago. YOU are wearing your hair curly because it's cute as hell. And I waited to tell you because I thought it'd be a nice surprise. It's going to be awesome, baby girl, stop making yourself nervous. I HATE when you do that."

I sit back down on the couch and can feel the worry in my face slowly wash away as I force myself to relax. My cousin's words marinate in my mind, kicking the unnecessary concerns off center stage like the Sandman on Showtime at the Apollo.

She's right. I also hate when I over-think.

I shouldn't let my childish nerves ruin my opportunity to be and have fun with the *SHE Inc.* girls. Tonight could even result in more than just a fun time, because when you're with the right people all of the right doors begin to open up. I can use this opportunity to imitate Melanie's hustle: networking and talking.

I can build connections and even possibly make a few new friends. Who knows, maybe I will have the time of my life and decide to follow in Melanie's footsteps to be involved in the party industry, as well.

This is what it is all about: Being open to all the different opportunities that could arise by making myself and my mind available to every option that comes my way.

"You're right, it will be awesome. White dresses, huh?"

Melanie steps back and takes a seat on the other side of the sectional. "Yes, little worry wart. So, I hope you're not on your period because that might be the opposite of awesome if you don't like the feeling of super-sized tampons."

I respond with a face of disgust. Our conversation is interrupted by the sound of Sabrina's door opening and her Spanish accent screaming at Miguel. Melanie turns the music down just a little lower so we can listen as Miguel yells back at her roommate. His voice gets louder as he makes his way up her hallway and closer to the living area.

"YOU ARE SO FUCKING INSECURE!" He manages to yell as Sabrina's door slams closed and he emerges out the hallway and into the living room before us. He pauses in the discovery of our presence and we study him as his loud words echo up and against the vaulted ceiling.

Awkward.

He flashes his perfect smile to mask the embarrassment of his anger and heads in our direction. "What's up, ladies?"

Melanie raises an eyebrow as he leans against the end of the couch, closest to her. "What's up with you, Miguel?"

"Sabrina is like a super spy or something... She is always finding a reason to argue. Mucho loco." He spins his finger in a circle around his ear, giving the "crazy" motion as he rolls his eyes towards Sabrina's hallway.

Melanie giggles, "You're the one who keeps giving her things to argue about. Maybe if you'd learn the definition of *monogamy* and put it into practice..." She smiles matter-of-factly at her suggestion.

"Ha!" Miguel licks his lips and returns a sly smile to his face. "Sabrina knows that I am a man. Men have needs. Maybe if she learned how to accommodate them instead of channeling all that energy into fighting with me when I mess up, we would be alright."

I laugh at Miguel's twisted logic and turn my attention to the view outside of the windows.

Melanie waves her hand at his words as if they are fruit flies. "Boy, I am not fooling with you right now, get out of here."

"No, no... Different topic," Miguel changes the subject, "You know I'm gonna be at the club tonight. It's supposed to be insane."

"Yeah, I already know you're gonna be there." Melanie says, spilling her confidence all over Miguel as if she knows any event that she hosts is the best place to be.

My phone vibrates as they continue to talk about the party, so I reach into the pocket of my hoodie and pull out the device, *Good morning. How are you feeling?*

My insides smile when I see Dylan's name at the top of the screen and I type a response.

"Is your one friend going to be there tonight? The one with the... You know." Miguel asks Melanie as he cuffs his hands around his chest to finish the sentence.

"No, I don't know, Miguel! I don't want anything to do with your shenanigans. If you want one of my girls you need to leave me out of it!"

My phone vibrates again, *That's good. I'm doing well too. What do you have planned for the day?*

Miguel laughs, "How do you know I'm asking for myself? I could be asking for a friend!"

Melanie returns a laugh oozing with sarcasm, not even entertaining his words with a rebuttal.

"Okay. You don't have to tell me because I'll see for myself, anyway."

Melanie shakes her head. "You are too cute to be this much of an asshole to your girlfriend."

"Well, maybe if your party girls weren't so hot I wouldn't be so tempted. Isn't this why they're so hot, though? To tempt men like me and my friends into giving them attention and coming out of our pockets?"

Another vibration, *Oh, cool, I'm pretty sure I'll be heading up there with Jay and the guys tonight. You're just going with Melanie?*

Melanie lets out a loud, aggravated sigh. "Okay, Miguel, you can exit my apartment now."

Miguel laughs and makes his way towards the door. "Alright, I'll see you ladies tonight."

I glance up from my phone to watch him leave and he winks at me as he opens the door and lets himself out.

What an extremely handsome douchebag.

AWAY

The door shuts and Melanie jumps up to head into the kitchen. "I'm about to fix us some breakfast, my stomach has been growling viciously for ten minutes and Miguel's presence just makes me nauseous."

Another vibration pulls my attention back down to my phone, *Oh you'll be an actual S.H.E rep tonight? Your cousin is letting you join that?*

I am confused by his message.

Is he questioning my cousin's decision to bring me into the group? My ability to be a "Bad Mama Jama" and party with the ladies? My response will reflect my newly found confidence in myself to hang with the big dogs.

He better recognize.

"Girl, tonight is going to be crazy! There is so much money to be made. There are, like, fifteen birthdays being celebrated. Ronald even flew in some of those Hawaiian, fire-eater dancing guys. Have you ever seen that before? Some guys eating some damn fire in the club? Ha!" Melanie continues to exclaim her expectations for the night and I watch as Dylan's next text message comes in.

Lol. I'm not saying you can't hang. I just… Wondered, I guess. Well, I'll see you later beautiful.

Nine.

Los Angeles, Present Day

High heels. Long legs. Tight white dresses.

It was just before midnight when Melanie and the eleven *SHE Inc.* representatives, including myself, were lined up in the front of Melanie's apartment building. Eyes fierce and bodies frozen in our sexiest poses as the group's photographer snapped away.

"You ladies always make my job so easy," He says as he maneuvers around the group, capturing the best views possible under the glimmer of the streetlights.

All of the women seem to radiate their beauty effortlessly, and everyone works together to achieve a successful photo shoot before the rides arrive to take us to the event of the night.

"Okay. I think we've got enough footage, Thomas. Thank you," Melanie steps away from the group, who remains lined up against the patterned wood exterior and windows of the building. "Just snap some candid shots for the next few minutes while we wait. Actually, let me see those images really quickly." Melanie stares into the camera with the photographer and the group of women disperse from their line, forming a talking and laughing cluster on the sidewalk. I stand back and study who I will be working with tonight.

Just like their varying ethnicities, some of them being Caucasian while others are African-American as well as Asian and Hispanic, their dresses are white as snow and glow in different styles. Some have on halter tops while others are sleeveless or off-the-shoulder, allowing the women to express their personal preferences by picking the style best suited for their bodies. Yet, everyone remains in-sync.

Their frames also range from thick and curvy to runway-model skinny, while some are 5'11" in their heels and others barely make it past 5'1", such as myself.

The beauty in diversity.

When Melanie strategically selected women of different ages, cultures, and sizes, she knew it would allow her business to reach a wider audience. If everyone in the group looked the same, they would have been limited to a niche market and would not have been extended as many opportunities for bookings. The group may have still been relying only on these club gigs to pay the bills. But since their target audience is much greater and they are filled with different viewpoints, styles, and business savvy, they have been able to expand successfully and reach numerous women in numerous areas with numerous backgrounds.

Strategy.

Conversations of excitement for tonight's festivities go on and I check my reflection in one of the windows before attempting to join in. I listened to Melanie and did not straighten my hair, but instead defined my natural, dark brown curls with water, coconut oil, and a decent amount of teasing to maintain the volume and make them sexier.

Hair: Check.

Melanie's makeup skills almost brought me to my knees. My eyebrows are naturally thick, but she cleaned them up to perfection. Subtle shimmers of gold eye shadow was applied to my eyelids and a strip of eyelashes glued on to dramatize my natural ones. My lips have been decorated with a nude lipstick that matches well with my light brown complexion.

Face: Check.

Fringe gold earrings shine on my ears as the clock necklace from Tiffany & Co. dangles around my neck.

Nude single-sole, open-toed heels are strapped onto my feet and my nude clutch with gold detail is grasped firmly by my freshly manicured hands.

Accessories: Check.

When Melanie and I arrived at the boutique to pick up our dresses, the only sizes that were left were in the off-the-shoulder styles, so that is what we are both zipped into for the night. My body is hugged by this dress in a way that I have never seen before. I am not an excessively curvy female, but it is giving the illusion that I am while my semi-flat stomach (I have been trying to get rid of the tiny pouch of stomach fat that I have had for years) and B-Cup breasts don't look half-bad.

Body: Check.

Nobody can tell me anything tonight.

"Tam, come here! Let me introduce you to everybody!" I turn around to find Melanie walking away from Thomas and toward the group, her hand in the air waving me over. Her skin is glowing under the streetlights in perfect contrast to her white dress, and her white teeth are shining through the smile spread across her face.

All eyes of the women turn and watch with curious eyes as I walk over to stand beside my cousin. She links our arms together as she always loves to do. "This is my baby cousin, Tamryn. Well, she's twenty-one so not much of a baby anymore, I guess," Melanie shrugs and I feel my cheeks flush as all of the ladies break out into giggles and aww's. "She recently moved here and will be joining our group!" Melanie finishes the introduction with an applause and the ladies follow suit.

Hugs, compliments, and introductions overwhelm me as everyone gathers around simultaneously trying to get to know their newest member.

I cannot help but to wonder if they are really this excited to meet me or if they are really good at trying to impress my cousin.

But, does it matter?

Whether their welcoming acts are genuine or fake, they all came together and had faith in this group for the sake of uplifting women. What good would it be if they did not practice what they preach? Or what good would it be to take part in a group that you do not truly believe in? For the free parties?

Hmm.

Maybe it's just their welcoming gestures are so different from what I am used to growing up. Females were always more willing to compete and put each other down, rather than finding happiness in lifting each other up. Beautiful ladies would come in contact with other beautiful ladies and their first reflex was to find something negative to point out about her.

Hate.

Now, here I am surrounded by some of the most gorgeous women I have ever seen and they are displaying more than their physical appearances. These women are showing me their personalities and their hearts and their willingness to show love as opposed to hate. So, instead of assuming it may all be fake or that they will roll their eyes and talk about me when my back is turned, I will allow their smiles to be as genuine as they appear.

A black 2015 Mercedes GL-Class SUV pulls up along the curb, followed by a silver 2016 Ford Explorer and all of the girls wait for the trucks to stop before preparing to hop in.

"I have to ride in the Mercedes! I am feeling WAY too sexy to not ride in luxury!" One of the ladies exclaim as she flips her hair and struts her tan legs toward the GL-Class.

"I'm feeling and looking sexy enough to make the Ford feel and look like luxury, sweetheart. I can show up to the club on a bike and still slay!" Says another one, swinging her hips towards the Ford truck and sending the rest of the women into a flurry of laughter as everyone splits to get into the different rides.

I follow Melanie to the Mercedes SUV and climb in the backseat with several of the other ladies while she hops in the front and talks to the driver. Once it is confirmed that all the women are in the vehicles, we pull out into the streets of Los Angeles and make our way to Ronald's *Illusion* nightclub.

Let the night begin.

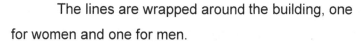

The lines are wrapped around the building, one for women and one for men.

Illusion is Ronald's newest venue, located on Hollywood Boulevard. Stars of the Walk of Fame rest underneath the six-inch pumps of glamorous women and fresh shoes of handsome men standing on the sidewalk. Everyone is dressed to impress and awaiting their turn to enter.

"Yeah, we just pulled up... Okay... Yes, babe." Melanie's phone is to her ear as she waits for the driver to open her door.

I am sure to focus on keeping my legs close together as I step down from the SUV in my dress. The last thing I want to do is give the line of people watching a show.

The ladies from the other truck walk over to us and all of the representatives begin to form a line, two girls side-by-side in front of two girls side-by-side and so on.

I figure this must be a signature entrance of theirs, so I stand out of the way and work hard to avoid looking out of place as I wait to be given direction as to where to go.

Melanie gets off the phone and stands at the head of the pack, analyzing the women carefully and making sure that everyone is ready to go inside. Her back is towards the entrance of the club, giving the men a view to drool over as they high-five and fantasize about the things they would do if they ever had a chance with her.

Once the analysis of the women is complete, Melanie's eyes flash in my direction. She moves a loose strand of hair from her bob to behind her ear before curling her red lips into a smile and motioning for me to come stand next to her.

Oh, boy.

I tighten the grip on my clutch as my palms begin to sweat. I can feel myself growing anxious, but I take my place at the front of the line with Melanie and pretend I do not notice the dozens of eyes watching our every move. The problem is I know my body language is saying otherwise.

Flashes from Thomas' camera begin again.

Melanie switches her red Marc by Marc Jacobs wallet to her left hand with her phone and takes a hold of my hand in hers. She looks down to me from her boosted height of 5'10", thanks to the white Giuseppe Zanotti "Cruel Summer" heels on her feet. "Are you okay, Tamryn?" She asks with a comforting gaze as she maintains that same smile. I'm forced to stop shaking in my heels from nervousness.

"I'm fine."

Melanie nods her head and directs her attention to one of the guards standing by the glass doors. He holds his hand up in the "okay" signal, letting Melanie know that our section is ready. "Good. You look gorgeous. I want you to let loose and have fun tonight." She straightens her face as she stares through the glass doors serving as the entrance into a long hallway with blue lighting that leads to another set of black doors that serve as the official entrance.

I take a deep breath, imagining that I'm inhaling some of her carefree confidence. Then I exhale out the shaky nerves of being in the spotlight. "Okay, I will."

"Good. Now, let's fuck this club up."

Melanie begins walking and we all stride passed the lines of people and through the glass doors being held open by the strong gentlemen in black suits that are in charge of guarding them. The same bouncer that gave us the signal is now speaking into his headset, "SHE reps are entering now."

The walls are lined with built-in aquariums that stretch all the way down the hall. The sound of our heels against the floor echo and bounce off the ceiling. Light from the blue bulbs above us and light from the aquariums shine a blue glare against our white dresses. I look closely at the fishes. But, squinting my eyes I realize that they are not real fishes. These are not aquariums built into these walls, but actually high definition flat screen televisions currently programmed to exhibit life under the sea.

Illusion.

We start to close in on the second pair of doors and, like clockwork, they are opened just in time for our arrival.

The strong bassline of a hip-hop song remixed into house music consumes our ears. My chest vibrates from the beat. The main part of the venue is a huge room, lined with navy blue leather couches and plush chairs with people standing on top of them from wall-to-wall.

The club is packed.

Some of the small tables in sections are already covered with champagne and liquor. Girls in black bodysuits are rushing through the crowd with bottles held high in the air and sparklers flaring.

There are three bars from what I can see in our quick commute across the room to get to our designated area; one by the door, another on the other side of the room, and one more in a separate part of the club that appears to be more of a lounge area.

It is just as dark in here as it was in *the Crawlspace*. Spotlights are moving throughout the crowd as well as colorful laser lights that shine across your face at least once every five seconds. There are also lights shining down from huge chandeliers hanging from the twenty-feet high ceiling, illuminating the club with different colors that are choreographed to the music. A smoke machine blows onto the dance floor as we drift passed in our line.

It is already better than any club I have ever been to in my life.

The section deemed as ours is a platform located at the front of the room about five steps high. Its right in front of the DJ booth, which is even more elevated with a huge screen on the wall behind it that switches between scenes of the crowd and random imagery, such as more fishes and the logo of the current DJ in charge of the tunes.

"The SHE Inc. ladies are in the building! Shout out to Mel-Moneybags!" The DJ yells into his microphone, followed by laughter as Melanie rolls her eyes with a fake smile.

"I told him to stop calling me that," She says through her teeth as we climb up the few steps to our section.

The line of representatives are still filing in to get settled on the long curved couch when three of the girls in bodysuits come dancing up the other set of stairs located on the other side of the platform. The bottle-girls have the biggest smiles on their faces and the first one is holding a bottle of Patron, the second holding a bottle of Moet lit up by an LED light, and the last is carrying a pitcher of orange juice in one hand and cranberry juice in the other. They cover the two tables in our area with the refreshments and persist to make sure we have everything that is needed including iced water, glasses, a tray of fruits, cheeses and crackers, and napkins. One of them head back down to cater to other guests while the other two stick around to pour drinks and fulfill anymore requests.

Mixed drinks, shots, and glasses of champagne are distributed amongst the ladies and we toast to a great night. There's no hesitation to join the party, most of the ladies immediately dancing on the couch and vibing to the bumping bass of the music.

AWAY

Ronald comes up into the section with his usual cool demeanor and he is tailored from head-to-toe. His gray suit is decorated with a red pocket square that compliments the red dress shoes on his feet.

He doesn't have to say anything in order for everyone to know that his outfit is expensive.

Melanie greets him with a hug and he plants a kiss on her cheek. Thomas and the club's photographer both snap away to catch the money-making duo that many have already assumed is a romantic couple.

Ronald's light brown eyes meet mine and he waves as he whispers something into Melanie's ear. I wave back as she nods her head in response before watching him turn around and head back down the stairs. Then she looks back to her group of ladies, half of them now sitting while the other half is still dancing. One of them motion for Melanie to sit next to her in the middle of the couch and Melanie motions for me to come with her.

So, with my clutch underneath one arm, a glass of Moet in one hand, and a glass of Patron mixed with orange and cranberry juice in the other, I follow my cousin to join her in the center of the group.

Everything is like a movie.

The drinks are beginning to quicken my heartbeat as we all laugh and dance to our favorite songs blasting through the speakers. The photographers continue to take pictures and their constant flashes make me feel famous. As well as being on the platform with these ladies above the rest of the crowded club.

Good-looking men are starting to file through our section, using their best lines to attract the ladies who all have drinks in their hands and smile coyly whenever one of the gentlemen say something in their ears.

Then a couple familiar faces appear.

Walking up one of the sets of stairs comes the same guy Melanie was networking with at *the Crawlspace* and his group of friends. Melanie stands to greet him with a hug and his friends monitor the area like hungry dogs surrounded by steaks.

I turn my head, landing my eyes on another gentleman talking to one of the representatives. He places a small plastic bag into her hand but I failed to see what was inside. I look back toward Melanie to find her shaking hands with the guy she was talking to before coming back to sit.

She keeps her eyes on him as he puts his finger in the air and I read his lips. *One hour.* He heads back down the steps.

"I told you tonight would be crazy!" Melanie says, turning to me and moving another loose strand of hair behind her ear.

"Yeah, you were right!" I yell over the music, blinking my eyes several times to shake the impending results of the several drinks I have had.

There are people everywhere. Not one couch or chair in the entire building can be seen without men or women standing or sitting on top of them.

The DJ announces the presence of a few Clippers players and singers. Then he shouts out the numerous birthdays being celebrated, giving rise to cheers from the various sections of the club from corner to corner with every name that is called.

I look back toward the girl in the group who was handed the plastic bag. One of her hands is holding a glass while the other is fixing her long brown hair as she rocks her body to the beat of the current song playing. There is no sign of anything like what I thought I had seen, so I conclude that I didn't really see anything.

Stop thinking so much, Tam.

Suddenly, the music changes from a pop song to a fury of drum sounds.

Spotlights above a second-floor balcony that I had not even noticed before are shut on and two muscular men with Hawaiian features appear. They're wearing black, shimmering shorts and grass boots, both holding one staff.

"Oooooh, look! The fire guys! There they are!" Melanie hollers like a six year-old at a circus as she taps my arm repeatedly to ensure that I'm watching.

The crowd goes crazy and the dancers give each other a nod before simultaneously lighting both ends of their staffs with palm torches and beginning their routine.

I join in with the cheers that are shaking the building, clapping and screaming for the dangerous entertainment bestowed upon us. The DJ mixes in a popular rap song by Future over the beat of the drums and the crowd goes even more wild. Everyone dances to the remix as they continue to watch the Hawaiians toss their burning staffs into the air while spinning round and catching them.

One of the bottle girls pours me another glass filled with tequila and juice.

Then Melanie stands, grabbing my hand to follow her and we step up onto the couch to start dancing with the other girls.

The alcohol and the club's dynamic atmosphere begin to take control of my body. My hips are moving sultrily, and I'm letting myself fall into the environment. Letting loose as my mind clears and I am released into a secret, bold and careless world located under the influence.

Welcome.

The fire-dancers finish their performance and bow in appreciation of the cheers before the spotlights shut off and the music changes into another popular song. The tone of the club is brought out of Hawaii and back to the Los Angeles club scene.

Then, more familiar faces.

Miguel is spotted coming into the section, followed by a few of his friends and I immediately glance at Melanie to find her eyes already focused on the cheating print model. He smiles at us as he extends a hug to one of the women in white.

That must be who he was attempting to ask Melanie about earlier.

I lean over to my cousin's ear, "You're going to let him talk to one of your ladies?"

"It's none of my business," She responds, putting the straw of her drink into her mouth and dismissing the topic. Her eyes are directed elsewhere.

A tap on my shoulder sends me turning in the other direction. A few of the ladies are looking at me as they smile and dance, one holding the zip-lock bag I noticed earlier. She reaches her hand out for me to take it, so I grab the plastic to discover its contents.

There are small pills of various colors with different pictures etched on them from smiley faces to crowns to hearts. I look back up, noticing each of the ladies holding one of the tiny substances and waiting for me to pick one.

Whoa.

I contemplate my next move.

Pop a pill with the cool kids? What if they find me rude for saying no? What if I embarrass myself? I have always wondered what the effects of an ecstasy pill were like, and I have never been the best at dealing with peer pressure...

I'm thinking too much again.

I extend the bag back to the girl and shake my head, declining politely.

The last thing I need is to end up like Smokey from "Friday", twitching and afraid in someone's pigeon coop. While my imagination may be wild in considering the most dramatic of outcomes, how sure can I be that whatever pill I grab out that bag will not have the same effects on my body that "Angel Dust" would have?

I'll pass.

The girl's green eyes sparkle with understanding, "Aw, you're a good girl! I love it!" She grabs the bag, handing it back to one of the other ladies. They all toast and pop the pills into their mouths, following up with alcohol while one washes hers down straight from the Moet bottle and finishes it off.

One of the bottle-girls take notice and run down the steps to grab another bottle of champagne for us.

The night goes on and I have attracted the attention of several gentlemen that Melanie introduced me to.

Scott, the real estate investor. Myles, the retired NFL player. Jake, the insurance specialist.

I was sure to save all offered contact information in my phone and maintain a sweet persona, but I already know that I will not be reaching out to any of them. They were all easy on the eyes, either draped in tailored suits or clean-cut casual wear as they asked if I was available. And they remained respectful when I answered no with an apologetic smile.

I cannot help the fact that Dylan is on my mind.

I wonder if he's still coming?

Yet, as much as I want to shoot him a text, I already know he would contact me on his own if plans had changed. Because as bad as I want to see him, I know he wants to see me more.

A guy approaches Melanie who appears to be around her age in his mid-twenties. She leans down to hear him from her standing position on the couch. I watch as he pulls a wad of money from the jacket of his suit and Melanie's hand pushes his hand of funds back into his jacket. Her other hand points at one of the ladies in a sleeveless, white dress standing at the end of the couch. He does a motion, with his free hand, as if he is pretending to smoke and Melanie laughs before shaking her head "yes".

The guy then shifts down to the woman that Melanie directed him to, proceeding to talk in her ear and run his fingers through his combed-back hair.

Words are exchanged and I stare, trying to read their lips until Melanie throws her arm around my shoulders. "You are so drunk!" She yells into my ear and her laughing sends me into a drunken hysteria of giggles with her.

"I'm having so much funnnnnn!" I yell back as I fall over my cousin and a hiccup pushes from my chest.

I glance back toward the end of the couch, hoping to finish spying on the conversation between the guy in the suit and the representative but they are no longer there. Another tap on my shoulder sends me swinging back around to the ladies who popped the pills.

The one with green eyes keeps her hand on me for balance as she hands me a glass of champagne. "Is that your real hair!? It is so pretty!" Her words are slurred and pupils dilated under her low eyelids. I briefly wonder if I look and sound as drunk as she does.

I take a sip from the glass and the black choker with a rhinestone in the middle that is wrapped around her neck catches my attention. I lean in to respond to her, "Thank you! I love your choker! My friend Dana has one just like it!"

The girl laughs at my compliment a little too hard. "Come dance with us!"

She pulls on my arm and the other ladies start to head down the stairs.

I turn around to let Melanie know, but she is already waving for me to go. So I turn back and follow the three ladies down into the crowded dance floor.

The gripping introduction of R&B singer, The Weeknd's hit single, "The Hills", blares through the speakers. The choreographed chandeliers dance shades of red as they are suddenly overpowered by the flashing of black and white strobe lights.

The illusion of everyone moving in slow motion through the fast blinking lights is strong. My alcohol euphoria is heightened. I keep my clutch squeezed tightly under my arm and quickly drink the rest of the champagne in my glass. 'Green eyes' maintains her grasp on me, making sure I don't get separated from the group.

We emerge into an open space in the middle of the dance floor and I wave the hand holding the empty champagne glass high in the air as I begin to work my body to the music. Everyone around us appears to be in a zone and we are no exception. The substances we have consumed have no plans of relinquishing our bodies anytime soon. The bass continues to vibrate my chest and I give in to its tickles, loving this entire feeling washing over me as The Weeknd's voice dances through my ears:

"*Hills have eyes, the hills have eyes,*

Who are you to judge? Who are you to judge?"

I forgot that the empty glass was still in my hand when 'green eyes' unexpectedly grabbed it, tossing it on the floor behind her. Our group erupts into laughter as it refuses to break, bouncing and sliding across the floor and only stopping when it hit the heel of a girl. A dirty look and rolled eyes are sent our way.

"*Arrogant whores… They're not even that pretty…*"

We are the lives of the party.

Dozens of eyes watch our dance movements closely and before I knew it, there were men coming from different directions. They brought their bodies in close, grabbing our hands to dance with them while others wait patiently for their chance.

We all had a different gentleman to vibe with to the music and every time the song changed, so did our dance partners.

Songs have come and gone, and so have many men.

I'm starting to feel as though we have been on the dance floor for hours. My body is hot and winded. Beads of sweat form over my face.

This dress feels a little too tight.

I unwrap the arms of a random gentleman from around my waist and give myself some time to breathe. He catches the hint and disappears into the crowd. The other women in white are still going strong, one practically having sex with her dance partner while the others dance all over each other.

All I can think about is water as my head starts to pound. My heart beating rapidly as though it wants to jump out my body. The strobe lights and red lasers no longer seem as cool, and the tickle I was feeling from the booming bass feels more like multiple punches to my chest.

I am officially out of it. This is the part of drinking where my inebriation has reached its peak and begins to spiral down like a roller coaster that is out of control. Upon realizing what is happening, my body begins to prepare for what happens next. My stomach is starting to turn.

Yep, the fun is over.

Shit.

"Are you okay, love?" One of the other *SHE* representatives grab my arm with a look of concern.

I attempt to pull myself together. I can't look as scared and sick as I am beginning to feel. "I'm fine. I just haven't been out like this in a while," I smile reassuringly. "I'm gonna see if there's any water left in our section."

She smiles back as my arm slips out of her grasp in the start of my commute. I slip through what seems like millions of moving bodies to get back to our designated platform. My feet wobble in my heels and I try to regain balance.

It would help if the room stopped spinning.

Just be cool, Tamryn. Get off this struggle bus and make it back to the section. Then you can drink some water and sit your ass down!

A strong grip around my waist pulls me backwards.

I spin around, falling into the chest of a Caucasian male probably in his early thirties. He has to be about 5'10" with an athletic build and black hair. I study his face as he leans in to my ear. Maybe he is one of the many people I was introduced to by Melanie tonight. "Can I have you, beautiful?"

I push away from his grasp, realizing I have never met this man in my life. Disgust covers my face from his nerve to have asked that question.

He pulls me back in, bringing me face to face with the alcohol on his breath. His eyes examine every part of my body located below my neck. "It's about time they added someone as sexy as you to the group. I've been watching you all night."

His words are ruthless to match his strong hold on me that doesn't seem to be letting up. I dig my manicured nails into the skin of his arm and he releases my torso, giving me just enough time to dip through the crowd in his moment of agony.

Reaching for the railing of the steps, I pull myself up. I'm back in the safety of our section, away from the abyss of the dance floor that appears to be swarming with perverts.

A fresh pitcher of water is sitting on one of the tables but all the glasses are used. So, I dump the small amount of champagne left in one glass onto the black marble floor and fill it with the iced water to quench my thirst.

My eyes scan the area to find that only three girls of the group have remained in the section.

Once again, Melanie is not where I left her.

I look around the club from where I stand, chugging the water like I had been stranded in the desert for weeks. The ice touches my lips after I swallow the final drops, so I reached into my clutch to grab my phone and text Melanie.

Two Unread Messages:

1:04 A.M: *Hey Young Tam, I'm here. Where are you?*

1:32 A.M: *Are you here?*

Dylan.

I try to respond but the light from the screen is threatening to take away my vision and possibly my life. The throbbing within my head emphasizes its presence, throwing my stomach back into flips and turns. My face flushes and my mouth begins to salivate.

Flight senses are activated in my brain as I realize I am about ten seconds from puking a mixture of liquor, champagne, cheese, and crackers all over the floor. Tossing my phone back into my clutch, I fight the urge to upchuck and strain to find a restroom sign from my position above the crowd. My eyes spot a neon one located on the other side of the club inside the lounge area.

Bingo.

Right hand over my mouth and left hand holding my clutch, I dive back into the crowd. It has become impossible to distinguish between the dance floor and the regular area due to the amount of people that are now dancing all over the place.

My short height and petite frame serve as an advantage as I squeeze between everyone. I maneuver beneath hands holding martini glasses and hope I'm not drawing much attention to myself. Small burps serve as threats from my body as they escape my lips. So I keep swallowing saliva repeatedly to hold off what is destined to happen and I finally reach the entrance to the lounge.

Running into the women's restroom and shoving by some unsuspecting ladies who were walking out, my body thrusts forward and the contents of my stomach make their big exit once I threw myself into the first stall.

Right on time.

Don't get it on your dress, Tam. Hold your hair back! Okay, you're done. Thank God. Wait… No, you're not!

After three releases of toxins that were upsetting my body, I can almost think clearly again.

There still seems to be two of everything in my blurred vision, but at least I'm not queasy and the headache isn't as strong. I kick my foot up to press the button that flushes the toilet and rest against the black stone wall, reaching back into my clutch to grab my phone and find out where the hell Melanie is.

Mel, I'm not feeling too good. Where are you?

Thank goodness for autocorrect.

The stall is bigger and cleaner than most bathroom stalls in nightclubs tend to be. The stone walls adding a contemporary touch and the white toilet appearing to have been scrubbed right before I threw up into it. I grab a piece of toilet paper from the dispenser and I close my eyes as I pat my forehead and upper-lip, trying not to cry.

The goal was to let loose and have fun tonight. Meet new people, drink, and live life. I have far exceeded that goal. I have lived my life so much this evening that it may be in danger. If I pass out and die from alcohol poisoning in this bathroom, I will be very upset as I float into the afterlife.

I dig around the insides of my clutch for a pack of gum. None. Why didn't I bring any gum with me? Oh yeah, Melanie has the gum. Where the hell is Melanie!?

I NEED YOU MEL, TEXT ME BACK!

I initiate a phone call. There are a few rings before it goes to voicemail. I click her name again and it goes to voicemail again. Another call... Voicemail. Another text... No response. Another call... Voicemail.

What is going on?

I take a few deep breaths in attempts to calm myself down and hold back the salty tears that are burning the back of my eyeballs. My body continues to sweat but I have chills. I begin to rue accepting that last drink.

That damn last drink that 'green eyes' handed me.

Even if I would have thought about it first, I probably would not have declined since I already declined their drug offer. I would not want them to think I was just here to decline all their party favors.

But, maybe they didn't like when I turned away the pills and decided to put one in my drink as payback.

And this is where the overthinking must end.

My phone remains in my hand as I stumble out of the stall and lean against the black marble counter of the sink. I rinse my mouth out with water from the tap, then make eye contact with my reflection in the large mirror. My shaking hands and blurred vision make it difficult to pull myself together, but after applying more lipstick and powdering my face I head back out into the lounge.

It is a little brighter in this area of the club. There are a couple pool tables, one of the bars, and televisions showing the same videos as the huge screen behind the DJ booth.

The last thing I want to do is go back into that crowd in the main room, but I need to find Melanie. I might even be okay if I find one of the other ladies of the group. But who knows how much of a help they would be all drugged up and just as drunk, if not drunker, than I am.

So here goes nothing.

I head back into the main room with haste, ready to find someone to protect me and my drunkenness but the mission is immediately interrupted. I trip right back into the arms of the creep from the dance floor, and he pushes me against the wall that is right outside the lounge. His strong grip proving too tough for me to challenge.

"Damn, we must be meant for each other," He laughs, his hands clasping tightly to my waist. "Quit fighting it."

"Oh my gosh, get the hell off me!" I try to peel his hands off my body, unsuccessfully. Maybe someone in the crowd will notice what is happening and save me.

His hands slide down the sides of my body and over my butt before squeezing on my upper-thigh. "You know you want this as bad as I do... I have so much money and all I want to do is spend it on you." His right hand digs up my dress and the fight senses of my brain are activated. I throw my knee into his groin, sending him toppling over and his grasp on me is released.

I escape back into the lounge area, glancing over my shoulder as I push through moving bodies to find one of his friends pushing through those same bodies and reaching for me.

Oh, goodness.

My heart skips and I wish I could just wake up from this nightmare to realize I am actually back at the loft asleep on my futon in Melanie's bedroom. I cannot figure out how this night became such a trainwreck where I am preparing myself to be captured by this man's extended hand. Then my body collides into a pair of open arms.

I face forward to find Dylan and he pushes me behind him as he comes face to face with the creep's friend.

"Is there a problem?"

The friend keeps his eyes on me as the creepy guy and their other partner come to his side. "Is that your girl?"

Jay and two other guys step up next to Dylan. Surrounding partygoers direct their attention to the potential fight that is about to erupt.

Dylan ignores his question. "I said is there a problem?" His fists are balled and a vein is visible through the tattoos on his arm, which lead up to the sleeves of his white button down shirt that he paired with khaki joggers and white Nike Huarache sneakers.

This "tough-guy" mode he has activated is tempting me, my drunkenness, and my puke-breath to jump on him.

The creepy guy grabs his friend's arm, urging him to leave it alone. "No problem here, man. Come on guys," They back away, and not until they disappear into the crowd does Dylan turn around to face me.

"What the hell was that, Tam? Are you okay?"

I wrap my arms around his body. The side of my face snuggles into his chest and I close my eyes to stop the room from spinning. My hormones are running wild. "No. I'm not okay, Dylan."

"Who were they? How much have you had to drink tonight?" He bends his head down so I don't have to yell over the music. But I fall quiet and take a deep breath of his cologne, allowing the scent with its usual hint of marijuana to calm my rushing heart.

I can only imagine how intoxicated I must appear for him to ask about how much I have been drinking.

"I can't find Melanie," I open my eyes as he guides me to a chair that one of his friends dragged over.

"What do you mean you can't find Melanie? You came here with her and the group right? Why the hell would they leave you fucked up and by yourself?" His voice is strong and caring as it speaks the truth.

Why would Melanie go missing in action and why would those girls even let me try to go back to the section alone? Have they not heard of the buddy system? What about the obligation of women to travel in pairs and packs while out and about at all times? For ladies who seem so concerned about uplifting and protecting the sanctity of women, they did not seem to think about my well-being as I wandered off drunk and alone.

I bury my face into the palms of my hands and feel the tears coming back. But, this time I let them squeeze through my eyelids and slide down the sides of my face. I have no more fight left in my body.

"Shit. Don't cry..." Dylan places a hand on my back and starts rubbing in small circles. I keep my embarrassed face hidden in my hands and cry even harder at the thought of how my makeup will look after this.

I hear Dylan ask one of his friends to grab me napkins from the bar and some water, then he wraps his arms around my body.

"I bet I know where her cousin is. You may as well take advantage of this blessing that has just fallen into your lap. Young Tamryn is clearly fucked up. I'm sure she'll let you hit too." Jay's voice says in a practical tone, followed by laughter. I feel Dylan's hand move from my body and placed back. A rush of silence comes over Jay.

I could totally live without being in the midst of Jay, the crazy pervert, especially after being preyed on by that other man all night.

"Do you want me to try calling Melanie, Tamryn?" Dylan says into my ear. I nod my head, telling him the code to unlock my phone as I hand it over.

The tears finally stop after minutes of Dylan calling and sending texts from my phone and his. Jay also tried to call my cousin from his phone a few times.

No answers. No responses.

I move my hands from my face and Dylan hands me a glass of water as he dabs at the tears on my cheeks with a napkin.

"Your makeup is a little clownish now with all of that crying, lush." He jokes, also handing me a piece of gum. All I can do is laugh and be grateful that his sense of humor is strong enough to make light of this weird situation and the obvious puke on my breath.

The lights in the main room cut on and the DJ brings his set to a close, letting everyone in the building know that the party is over.

My phone rings in Dylan's hand and he answers it.

"This is Dylan, Mel... She is super drunk... We've been trying to get a hold of you... By the bathrooms..." He moves the phone from his ear to look at the screen, "She hung up. I think she's meeting us here."

A few minutes pass and Melanie emerges from the dissipating crowd. Her makeup is still flawless and a look of confusion sprawls across her face at the sight of mine all ruined. "Tamryn, what happened?"

I watch as she stares at Dylan questioningly. "I have been trying to find you all night. Where did you go?"

All eyes are on Melanie as she shifts her weight from one foot to the other. She raises an eyebrow. "I was in our section all night, Tam. I knew I shouldn't have let you drink that much. Come on, baby girl, let's go home," She reaches her hand out and I grab it as I stand up from the chair.

Home. Yes, please.

Dylan grabs my other hand, bringing our exit to a pause. "Call me when you wake up in the morning, Tamryn." His voice is stern but sweet. I force a smile before reaching up to plant a small kiss on his cheek.

"Thank you." I say before waving goodbye and following Melanie.

As we make our way out of the lounge, through the bright main room of the club and into the long hallway of HD televisions, I lag a little behind my cousin.

My eyes remain fixated on the back of her head and I am lost in thoughts spinning through my mind just like my vision.

We climb into the back of our ride that was waiting outside on the curb, and I close my eyes to banish the events of this terrible night from my brain. But, one thing keeps poking at my thoughts until I drift to sleep in our commute back home.

I am unable to forget about it. I am unable to ignore its obnoxious nagging as it kicks down the door to my mind and gets comfortable. Mocking me.

It's not the creep and his friends or the plastic bag of colorful pills or my puking alone in the bathroom.

"I was in our section all night, Tam..."

Ten.

Los Angeles, Present Day

Fireflies dance and float against the deep black sky like small orbs of light, leaving trails of stardust in their wake.

I blink and the creatures disappear into the darkness, being replaced by the silent explosions of fireworks. They flash yellow, green, and orange until the black sky swallows them up as I scrunch my face from a painful throb coming from my temples.

I force my eyes open, bringing the show underneath my eyelids to a close. Wiping the sleep away, I work to clear my vision while the sharp pounding inside my head grows greater.

There is a white bed sheet wrapped around me and the first sight I have awakened to is a black, steel banister. The white walls and high ceilings of the living room can be seen passed it, brightly lit by the sun that is high in the sky and shining through the floor-to-ceiling windows.

Too much light.

I come to realize that I fell asleep on the small loveseat located at the top of the black, winding staircase that leads to the loft area of the apartment. The loft area that I had never even stepped foot in during my stay, until now. The loft area that no one has probably stepped foot in for a while.

My phone is vibrating.

I follow the noise with my eyes, finding the device plugged in and resting on the papasan chair that is located by the outlet. My body hits the floor with a *thud* when I unsuccessfully tried to roll myself off the couch as gently as possible to crawl over and grab it.

The time flashes across the screen: *12:53 PM.*

Three Missed Calls. Two Unread Text Messages. One Voicemail.

I cannot say that I'm surprised about my sleeping in this late. I would continue to sleep for the rest of the week if it would free me of this hangover and delete the events I can still recall from last night out my memory.

My eyes squint as I check the unread messages from my position on the floor. A text from Melanie reads,

I ran to the store to grab some food and Gatorades. Forced you to swallow some Advil last night and there's more in my bathroom. You're not gonna feel too good when you wake up!!

You don't say?

The other text is from Dylan, *Just making sure you're still alive.*

Barely.

Melanie also called me twice and the other missed call is from an unknown number that also happens to be the phone number next to the voicemail notification.

I click to listen:

"Hello, this message is for Tamryn Bryant. My name is Courtney and I am calling from Mickey's Coffee Shop located in the Hollywood & Highland Center. I was looking over your application and would love to schedule a day and time for us to meet and talk about the Barista position for which you have applied. If you're still interested, you can reach me at…"

Well, I got an interview.

Bags can be heard being set down in the hallway right outside the apartment. I stare down through the caged banister as the door is opened and my cousin appears.

Melanie picks up about six plastic bags filled with groceries and wobbles into the apartment, tapping the door closed with the bottom of her black Nike Air Max sneakers. She is wearing a black tank top and blue jean shorts, so I could see the muscles in her arms flexing during her struggle to unload the weight of the grocery bags onto the breakfast bar in the kitchen.

She wipes her brow with the back of her hand and looks up, spotting my eyes on her from my sniper position in the loft. "I didn't want to make two trips from the garage. So yes, I carried all the bags up at once. And since you were too busy being in a drunken coma to answer the phone, I hope you still like blueberry pancakes."

<hr />

Shortly after my cousin returned, I went into the bathroom to take some medicine and peel off the white dress I still happened to be wearing.

The tan walls have grown used to sweating from my long hot showers and I felt so much better after turning Melanie's bathroom into a sauna. I could feel myself sweating out the remaining alcohol and toxins that were left in my system as I created an extreme lather of my body wash and scrubbed any memory of last night off my entire body.

Leaving Melanie's room in a clean white sweater and black leggings with my freshly washed hair tied back in a bun was like a rebirth of sorts. There has been one other time in my life where I got extremely intoxicated but it doesn't even compare to the level I was on at *Illusion* last night. I have never even endured a hangover until this morning and it feels as though my body has been building up with anticipation over the years, just waiting to unleash the harsh symptoms once it finally caught me ignoring my drinking limits.

I will never let this happen again.

The aroma of pancakes and bacon fills my nostrils as I get closer to the kitchen and as much as I wanted to enjoy it, my body teased with the possibility that it might just release any food right back out as soon as I take it in. With any luck, I should be able to eat again by Easter.

Melanie was putting the last slices of bacon on her plate when she noticed my entrance into the room. She points to a plate already prepared for me on the breakfast bar with an ice blue Gatorade sitting next to it.

I take a seat in front of the meal and crack open the magic hangover reliever to allow its electrolytes to relieve me of the sickness. She brings her plate to the other side of the breakfast bar in front of me to begin coating her pancakes with margarine while still standing.

"My crazy baby cousin, you owe me a HUGE 'thank you'," Melanie begins, urging me to watch her speak as I come up for air from chugging the Gatorade. "Do you remember anything that happened last night?"

A massive confusion takes over as I notice that I do not remember a single thing after leaving the nightclub and getting into the car. I shake my head and force a nervous smile as I brace myself for whatever she is bound to say next.

"Well… Just like I carried those heavy ass groceries, I practically had to carry you into this apartment last night… With my heels still on. Once I opened the door, you pushed away from me and darted into the bathroom like a bullet. Then you threw up in the toilet," A smile slips through Melanie's lips and she shoves a small pancake square into her mouth.

She chews, swallows, and continues the story.

"I held your hair back and almost puked with you when the smell hit my nose. Then, when you finally finished I stood you at the sink and made you rinse your mouth out with mouthwash, but instead of spitting it into the sink you spit it onto my dress."

I chuckle mildly at the thought and pick at the pancakes sitting in front of me with the fork in my hand. I really wish I could eat right now.

Melanie goes on to tell me how after I spit out the mouthwash, she helped me swallow a couple of Advil pills in an attempt to ease the expected headache of the coming morning. Then washed the makeup off my face while she dealt with my whining and crying as I kept trying to fall asleep on the bathroom floor. When she tried to get me to take off my dress I pushed away from her again, running out the bathroom and into the living room before climbing up the spiral stairs to the loft.

By this point she had given up, so she brought me a blanket, plugged in my phone, and went back down to her room to go to bed.

"You were like a little demon. I'm never letting you drink again, Tam. You are on punishment." Melanie points her finger in my face and we laugh. But my mind wanders back onto the issue that plagued my thoughts the moment before I passed out in the backseat during the ride home.

"Mel, you said you were in the section the entire night... Why didn't I see you when I came back up there from the dance floor?" I try to keep my voice as un-accusatory as possible. I don't want her to know that I think she lied, but the urgency of getting the answer to this question is unbearable.

I study her face as she bites a slice of bacon. So unfazed. So carefree.

So Melanie.

Keeping her eyes on the food, she answers. "Ronald needed me to come to his office for a second at one point during the night. We probably just missed each other," She ends her reasoning with a smile signifying innocence as she meets her eyes with mine. Another piece of pancake is stuffed into her mouth.

Game on.

"So, why did you say you were in the section all night when you weren't?" My voice touches on accusatory this time, but I can't help it. Why does it seem like she is lying to me?

"Because I basically was, Tam. I only left for, like, two seconds."

"You didn't see any of my texts and calls though?"

Melanie spreads a bigger smile across her face. An act that only someone as close to her as myself would know is a technique to hide how irritated she's becoming. My interrogation has brought her to the stage right before a volcanic eruption, but she tilts her head and lets out a sigh before responding calmly. "Tamryn. I saw the messages once I checked my phone at the end of the night and that is when I called you back and Mr. Dylan answered. I came straight to you! And while we are on this topic, Dylan is cute and all but why do you keep taking these risks with him? First at Jay's show and then last night while you were dead drunk? I know I said there's nothing wrong with expanding your focus, but what makes you trust this guy so much?"

Here we go with the trust issue B.S.

"If I didn't run into Dylan last night who knows what would have happened to me. He made sure I was okay after your group members let me wander off alone and YOU were M.I.A. Plus, I think those girls may have put something in one of my drinks. Something about my body did not feel right at all and it couldn't have just been caused by the alcohol." The memory of the cold sweats I had in the nightclub's bathroom give me goosebumps. I sip some of my Gatorade.

Melanie laughs. "Wow, YOU are just making up stuff now. When could they have put something in your drink, Tamryn? We were right next to them the entire time. And do you think I would have you around people that would do something like that to you? Really? You were drinking like a fish and you're like three feet tall, what you felt in your body is called 'repercussions'. And I was not M.I.A... It was just a weird mishap."

"I'm just saying, since you are so concerned about who I trust and the 'risks' I take. I do not really trust those girls. Last night wasn't right at all and there were so many little things that I picked up on that just seemed... Suspicious. I don't know..."

Melanie takes another bite of her pancakes. "Yeah, maybe you don't know. But okay, you're entitled to trust whoever you want. Since last night was so terrible, I cannot help but wonder if maybe the universe was giving you karma for when you worried me at the concert."

With that ridiculous insinuation, I decided to squash the discussion.

This conversation will go nowhere and do nothing but get worse. If Melanie does have a reason to be lying to me about being in the section, she does not seem to be planning on letting me figure out what that reason may be anyway. And if her representatives did do something to my drink, voicing my concerns is clearly not going to make a difference.

So forget it.

I change the subject. "A lady from the coffee shop I applied to called me this morning. I'm going to call her back and set up an interview." It may be safe to say that I will not be working another event with the *SHE* representatives for a while if ever again. This barista position will ensure that I do not have to.

Maybe I can't hang with the big dogs like I thought. Maybe I no longer care to.

"That's nice," Melanie's voice is dry as she walks over to the black leather purse on the other side of the counter. She digs inside for something.

"Yeah," I ignore her apparent carelessness of the good news. "I wasn't expecting to get any calls from any of those places, especially so soon. I guess I-," My words are interrupted as Melanie pulls a white envelope out of her purse and tosses it across the counter. It lands right next to my plate. I open it and a small stack of money is waiting inside.

"That's your cut from last night. Thanks again for coming out with us. I apologize that it did not end up being the greatest experience for you, but I really did enjoy having you there with me... No matter what you may think."

I finger through the bills. $600.

All of this money from one night of partying? No wonder Melanie can afford this apartment and her sports car and her expensive wardrobe. If this is just my cut, I can only imagine how much she tends to walk out with.

"Are you even going to eat the food that I cooked, Tamryn?" Melanie scolds me, noticing that I have yet to take a bite of anything on my plate. She reaches for one of my slices of bacon as I shake my head no.

The headache has completely subsided, thanks to the medicine and Gatorade. But, even if I wasn't suffering from this alcohol-induced sickness, my appetite would have been ruined by this conversation. Excluding the part with the money.

---◆---

I called Dylan back and he suggested that we get something to eat and hang out at a private beach a friend of his has access to. Miraculously, when he picked me up a couple hours later I was not as reluctant to food.

My body was practically begging for it.

I slip off my sandals as my orange sundress blows in the breeze with two ice cream cones and a basket of french fries in my hands. Dylan takes off his sneakers and socks, rolls up the bottom of his jeans, then reaches to get his ice cream cone back as we step into the warm sand. The sun beams down on us and our stroll on the beach begins as we head toward the glistening ocean washing against the shore.

The beach is quite small and I was surprised to see only a few families around with it being a Saturday afternoon. Then I recall how only residents of the gated community are permitted (or people who pretend to be residents with the parking pass from their friend who is a resident displayed on their rear-view mirror) as well as what Melanie mentioned about people around here and the winter months.

The weather is beginning to feel a little chilly as the sun prepares to set soon. Distant giggles of children playing in the sand and the ocean brushing lightly against the shore are the background noises to Dylan and my conversations. Our words escaping between bites of french fries and the diminishing of our ice cream cones.

We did a full recap of last night. I told him everything that happened from the photo shoot outside the apartment to the moment that I bumped into him, even though he begged for mercy when I went into vivid detail of my puking episode in the bathroom stall.

"I was just thinking you were having a really great time when you didn't text me back," Dylan shakes his head with a sympathetic smirk on his face. "Not being terrorized by some older guy and throwing up in the bathroom."

"Yeah... I was miserable. And had no gum." I dip a fry into the bit of ice cream left in my cone and toss it into my mouth. This is my first meal of the day after thinking I would not be able to tolerate any food for a while, and it could not be any better.

Dylan laughs. "Oh, I know. That's why I gave you some. Now it makes sense why your breath smelled so terrible."

I let out a sarcastic laugh and throw my arm out to punch him as my face flushes with embarrassment. He dodges my swing. "Let's change the subject."

We decide to anchor ourselves in a perfect spot as close to the water as we can get without being touched by it.

Once our bodies are settled onto the dry sand, I dig my toes into it and stare out into the ocean. The waves rushing against the shore and the vastness of the body of water begins to consume all of me: my mind, my emotions, my senses.

My fascination with the ocean is almost as strong as my love of sunrises and sunsets. I even used to love staring at Lake Erie when I was back home. The mystery contained within bodies of water is unimaginable, and the awareness that the land of the world is severely a minority in comparison blows my mind.

It is possible to humble anyone by making them stare out into the ocean or one of the Great Lakes or even the sky. You realize just how small you really are. All your issues might seem like huge deals from an automatic, everyday perception, but when you place them beside the beauty and mystery of nature, the things that really matter become clear.

My thoughts are running aimlessly, as always. I am unaware of the blank look upon my face as I stare out into the sea until Dylan waves his hand in front of my eyes.

"Hello… Are you still in there, young Tam?"

I giggle as I'm brought back down to Earth. "Shut up. It's just so beautiful."

Dylan nods his head in agreement and glances at the ocean to see what I see.

And I can see him thinking about something. He stuffs the last of his ice cream cone into his mouth and moves the camera hanging from the strap around his neck out of the way, then he reaches into the pocket of his jeans.

A little bag of his favorite green leafy substance is pulled out with a lighter and a small glass pipe. As he begins to carefully place the contents of the bag into the bowl of the pipe, he opens his mouth to speak. "So, Tamryn… Tell me what you care about."

Pardon?

I do not hide the confused expression on my face as I try to understand to what extent does he expect me to answer this question. "What do you mean?"

He flicks the lighter and the fire blares as he puts the pipe to his lips and burns the inside of the bowl. After a few puffs of smoke and his normal hold and exhale, he returns to the conversation. "At the concert you told me that you dropped out of school because you were studying a major that you didn't care about. So, what do you care about? What is your passion?"

Why is your memory so well?

I smile at the fact that he even remembers that conversation, but inside I am struggling with how to provide an answer to, yet, another question that I do not know the answer to. It would be so much easier to tell him *who* I care about or what I do *not* care about. My passion is something that has yet to be determined.

"I don't know," are the only three words I could muster.

"What would you do for the rest of your life if money did not exist?" He flicks the lighter and takes another hit from the pipe. His big brown eyes glisten behind the smoke that is blowing away in the gentle breeze.

I would probably sleep.

"I'm still trying to figure that out, I guess."

"Do you wanna start out as a SHE rep, then work your way up and become a video vixen? Is your dream to have one million followers across all your social media accounts one day?" Dylan jokes and pulls up the sleeves of his gray zip-up hoodie, revealing the tattoos that are decorating the inside of his forearm and a small name in cursive script that I had not been able to notice before.

Cheyenne.

That must be his sister's name.

"Hmm. You're very funny. But since money does, indeed, exist I actually have an interview at a coffee shop on Tuesday. So, maybe I can be a performing barista. I'll stand on the bar and pour shots of caramel mochas into everybody's mouth for the rest of my life."

"That would be pretty cool," Dylan flashes his smile and extends the pipe out towards me.

I stare at the shiny black glass and figure *why the hell not?*

His jaw drops as I accept the pipe and put it to my lips. "Can you light it for me?"

Dylan flicks the lighter and tilts it sideways to allow the fire to burn the inside of the bowl. I breathe in deep until my lungs are filled, holding my breath for just a few seconds before blowing the smoke out toward the ocean.

"You know, maybe you could help me out with something in the meantime of trying to find your passion. I love any opportunity to build my portfolio and you would be the perfect model for a concept I've been thinking of."

I raise an eyebrow to his proposition. "Aw, does Dylan want me to be his muse?" He steals a french fry from the basket and tosses it at my face so quickly I couldn't even react until it already bounced off my forehead. A laugh bursts through my lips. "No need to get all sensitive, I was kidding. I would love to help you with that! I've never modeled before, though."

"That's even better. You'll love it."

I smile and turn my head back forward to the ocean, noticing that the sun has lowered. All those magical colors are beginning to paint the sky and I hit the pipe two more times before deciding that should be enough.

We sit in silence besides a couple comments about seagulls in the distance and the cool breeze getting a little uncomfortable. He unzips his hoodie and drapes it over my cold shoulders.

My sweet friend Dylan.

"So, I'm just wondering... How old was your sister when she passed away?" I ask cautiously, the tattoo on his arm bringing the question to my mind.

Dylan's demeanor remains unfazed and he answers quite quickly. "Dominique was thirteen. Why?"

Dominique?

I mask my sudden confusion with a smile, "No reason."

Staring at the tattoo, I assume that *Cheyenne* must be Dylan's mother.

I look up at his face. His eyes are on mine, then they glance down at his forearm. "Oh, you thought Cheyenne was my sister's name. I see." He licks his lips and shifts his body, suddenly appearing tense.

"Yeah."

"We're friends right?"

"Yeah." I repeat.

A shy smile creeps onto Dylan's face. "Cheyenne is my ex."

"Oh." I face forward toward the ocean trying not to be awkward.

"A mistake I have yet to cover up."

"Believe me, you don't have to explain. It happens!" I playfully press my fist to his cheek. Dylan laughs and his body loosens back up.

More silence follows. The few families that were out have taken their children inside.

"Look, Tam," Dylan turns toward me, his eyes low and his face stern. I hope he doesn't say something else about Cheyenne. "I may be out of place saying this, but I wouldn't feel right if I didn't say anything."

Oh, boy.

"You should be careful around those girls in Melanie's group."

The water seems to brush against the shore a little slower and more lucid as the effects of smoking begin to kick in. It almost feels like my butt is floating right above the sand instead of digging into it. "What makes you say that?"

"Just be careful being associated with them. I've heard some things..."

"What kind of things?" I watch as Dylan averts his eyes. The wheels of his mind are turning. I am leaning on every impending word that is preparing to come out his mouth.

"Things that you may want to talk to your cousin about. Just be careful. I don't like the way I found you last night. I don't even understand how Melanie could let that happen."

He's right.

But he does not know about the talk I had with Melanie earlier. I have learned my lesson in regards to voicing my suspicions to my cousin about her and her group. Even if I did attempt to pull the truth out her again, this time my questions would be based on rumors heard by Dylan. There is no way I would acquire any worthy answers.

I'm over talking about it.

I shrug my shoulders and a chill runs down my body as I stuff the last of my ice cream cone into my mouth.

Dylan places his arm around me. "One more thing... Did she ever tell you where she was when you were looking for her?"

"Melanie said she was in the section the whole time, except when she went to Ronald's office for a minute. We probably just missed each other."

I'm ready for this conversation to end. I wish marijuana was like the *Red Bull* energy drink and gave you wings. I would sprout those suckers and fly into the sunset, as far away as possible from all of these secrets and paranoia that I am suddenly buried under.

Dylan's smile now seems forced but at an attempt to be comforting. "Yeah... Ya'll probably did just miss each other."

Eleven.

Cleveland, 2001

All the lights were off in Shannon's house.

The television dimly lit the living room, scenes from a late-night broadcast flashed across Travis's face as he slept. His body sat upward and head rested against the back of the couch.

Travis didn't like the idea of Melanie having to sleep in the house alone during nights that Shannon worked, so he began staying over. Just to make sure the twelve year-old girl he had started to take a liken to was safe and protected.

Most times he brought TJ with him.

The sixteen year-old usually had basketball practices to get to early in the morning before school, and sometimes Travis would give TJ's friend and teammate, Joseph, a ride to the school with them. So both boys would stay over, Shannon having the third bedroom comfortably set up for them. TJ slept in the bed and Joseph on a pile of comforters laid out on the floor.

This was just one of those regular nights.

It was a little after two in the morning when Melanie was awakened from her sleep.

The sound of multiple footsteps right outside her bedroom door is not an unfamiliar sound. The hard wood floors always *creak* whenever someone walks by. At this time of night, she usually knew exactly who it was.

So, Melanie rolls over under the plush lime green covers of her twin-sized bed growing anxious.

Tap, tap, tap… Tap, tap. The secret knock.

She crawls out of bed and placed her feet on the floor lightly, avoiding too many *creaking* wood sounds. Careful not to wake up Travis as she tip-toed to the door to let TJ into her room.

He closed the door and walked toward Melanie's bed to sit, then reached for the lamp sitting on top of the nightstand. The room is brightened before Melanie could prepare her sleepy eyes and she rubbed them with irritation while sitting down next to TJ. She pulled the bottom of her oversized white t-shirt down to cover her white panties.

"What's wrong?" She whispered. TJ leaned forward, wearing a black long-sleeved shirt with gray sweatpants and rested his elbows on his knees.

"I know what you said," He begins. "But I can't help the way I feel."

Melanie tugged at his shoulder for him to face her. "I feel the same way, T... But we have to stop... This isn't right."

TJ sat back and scooted closer to Melanie, his hand placed on the inside of her thigh and giving a squeeze. Melanie's insides jump. He leaned in to kiss her and she turned her head, forcing him to reroute his lips to the side of her neck.

The kisses he planted are soft. They reminded Melanie of the long nights they have spent talking and doing just this while her aunt was at work. Travis slept obliviously in Shannon's bedroom down the hall or downstairs on the couch.

"Where is Travis? Is he downstairs?" Melanie's thoughts made her heart skip from the apprehension that Travis could catch on to what they've been up to.

"Yes," TJ says between kisses. "Joe is right outside the door, he'll make a noise if he hears my dad wake up."

Melanie's mind raced as her hormones rage out of control.

The relationship between her and TJ has grown extremely complicated. They had become more and more inappropriately intimate over the past few months. The brother she never had has transformed into her first love, and as much as she wanted to continue to sneak around and enjoy the feelings that they shared she knew this had to end.

Her Aunt Shannon had begun to open up to her more and Travis continued to illustrate his commitment to them as much as he could. After all the prayers and wishes over the years, as well as envying Tamryn with her parents who would do anything for her, Melanie was finally able to enjoy having a family of her own. Being surrounded by people she could trust. People who showed concern and caring for her well-being.

Nothing was forced or out of pity.

How could she risk destroying the one thing that she had always wanted for TJ? This puppy love that should have never commenced. Yet, a bond she would hate to break.

It always seemed as though life could never be smooth sailing. There was always a catch.

She shoved him off her, bringing a halt to the kisses as she got off the bed to stand in front of the mirror above her dresser. Staring at TJ's reflection behind her, she watched as he remained seated on the bed looking at her with a look of perplexity. It almost made her uneasy.

Why can't he just understand?

"TJ, please. There are so many other girls you could be with. Everyone at your school loves you. What do you think can really happen with this? My Aunt and Travis will get married and we'll keep being together, secretly, forever? You think we'll never get caught?" She carefully retained her hushed tone, careful not to raise her voice but sure to emphasize every word. She had to ensure they will make it through the thickness of TJ's head.

He hopped up from the bed and stood behind Melanie, bringing her into a warm embrace and she fought the urge to melt into his arms, remaining stone cold.

"I don't want any other girls. I love you, Mel. We won't have to keep being together, secretly... We can figure something out."

I love you, Mel.

Melanie's eyes began to fill with tears as his words brought her back to the first time he ever spoke those exact words a couple months ago. It was the first time anyone had ever said that they loved her, besides Tamryn who was taught to say that to every family member.

They may be young, but Melanie knew what she and TJ had was real.

If it was under different circumstances, they could have grown up together and fell in love the right way. She could have been his date to homecoming for his senior year, when she would finally be a freshman in high school.

He could have been her first.

But this was not under different circumstances and the risks associated were too great. She needed to choose the larger possibility of a reward that would continue to last long into the future when this situation would, more than likely, be nothing but a distant memory of the past. Melanie chose a family.

Once again, she broke away from his grasp and kept a decent amount of space between them as she turned to face him. "I can't do this, TJ. You have to get out my room."

He stared back at her with his light eyes for what felt like an eternity before stepping back into her personal space. His hand reached up to fiddle with one of her two cornrows draped in front of her shoulder and he smiled to himself. "Do you really want me to get out?" He asked before kissing Melanie right on the lips, not giving her a chance to dodge it.

"Yes." She said, keeping her lips still in hopes that TJ will just take his final kisses in accepting her final decision. He had always been stubborn and strong-willed, two characteristics that always seemed to draw her into him until this moment.

Eyes closed, TJ continued to kiss Melanie's lips in hopes that she will give in. In hopes that she realizes she is not thinking clearly and has made the wrong choice. His kisses will reminded her that they were brought into each other's lives for a reason. He wanted nothing to do with any of the girls at his school because he is too focused on Melanie. The girl that had always been there for him and allowed him to be there for her. The only one who had understood the pain of living without a mother.

How could she ever want to break this up?

He kissed harder when she doesn't budge, holding her lips in place tightly and allowing him to put in all of his effort while she did nothing.

TJ opened his eyes as he stopped trying to break her down with kisses and pulled his face away from hers. The tip of Melanie's chocolate nose displayed a hint of red. It always did that when she's about to cry.

He refused to let her fight against this. He refused to let her fight against *them*.

"I don't think you know what you want," TJ pushed Melanie gently, but hard enough for the back of her legs to bump into the bed. Her body falls on top of the lime green comforter.

"TJ, I told you what I want and that is for you to stop playing and get out my room. Quit being dramatic." Melanie goes to stand back up, but TJ climbs on top of her, weighing her body down as he pulled his shirt over his head.

What is he doing?

Melanie's heart went haywire against the inside of her chest as she tried to understand what could possibly be going through TJ's mind right now. She reached up to push him off her but he pins both of her arms down over her head with one hand. The other hand reaches under her shirt.

He smiled. "Shhh…"

TJ's actions had the alarms sounding within Melanie's head, but his touches still had a way to melt her. She knew that what he was doing was crazy, but somehow, she looked in his eyes and could still see love.

"T, please stop… You're kinda scaring me right now." The octave of her voice was no longer in a hushed tone and he forced her to be quiet by pushing his lips back into hers.

The hand under her shirt started to pull down her panties and Melanie's whole body began to tremble in fear.

She wanted to scream.

But something deep within had convinced her that TJ would never have the intent to hurt her. Then there's the pain Travis would feel in running up the stairs to discover that his son could be capable of something like this.

It was almost as unimaginable as the pain she was feeling while experiencing it.

TJ had pulled Melanie's panties down to her knees and she begged him to stop as he reached into his sweatpants. "No, T... TJ... TJ, please..."

Tears rolled down Melanie's face as he ignored her words. So she decided to stop fighting.

Maybe she was prolonging the act by trying to make it end. Maybe if she stopped struggling he could just get it over with and this would all go away.

She just wanted all of this to go away.

The pressure began to penetrate between her legs, unleashing a sharp pain that turned Melanie's finger tips white as the blood was unable to flow due to her gripping the covers of the bed so hard.

"I love you, Mel... I love you so much..."

This was supposed to be just one of those regular nights.

"Is Melanie ready for school?"

Shannon just pulled into the driveway, catching Travis, TJ, and Joseph on their way out the house.

"I didn't hear her moving around so I called to her through the door," Travis gave Shannon a peck on the cheek, rushing to follow after the boys down the driveway to his truck parked across the street. "She said she's not feeling too well, babe. Let me know if you need me to grab her anything from the store."

The guys pulled off and Shannon went into the house, relieved to be home from another long night of work. She put her purse down, slipped off her shoes, and filled a glass with ice water from the refrigerator. She assumed her niece stayed up late listening to music again and was perfectly able to go to school today.

Shannon climbed the stairs with the glass of water in her hand and calls through Melanie's door. "Mel! Come on, girl. Get on up!"

She waited for a moment. No response.

"You have to get ready for school! Do you really not feel well!?"

Nothing.

"Are you asleep?" Shannon cracked open the door, "Your bus will be here in-,"

The glass of ice water slipped through her fingers and shatters against the hard wood floors. Shannon was face-to-face with the view of Melanie lying curled up on top of her bed. Blood is staining the lime green cover and the bottom of her niece's white shirt as she sobbed silently with her hands between her legs.

Twelve.

Los Angeles, Present Day

I had the Uber driver drop me off about a block away from the apartment building.

The interview with Courtney went well and I cannot keep my composure as I skip down the sidewalk under the clear blue sky. Landing this job has solidified my spot as an official living, working young woman of California. Proof that I don't need to hide underneath my cousin, as well as relieving me of the pressure of having to spend another night out and about with the *SHE Inc.* representatives ever again.

I am moving out of the "visitor" role and being able to be seen as a contributing member of the household. A right of passage, if you will. It makes everything about this move feel so much more... Real.

To accompany my beautiful and confident mood, I decided to check out the neighborhood that I have been calling my own for the past week. There is a cute cafe around the corner from our apartment, a pet shop a couple buildings down called "Buff Your Pup" (I imagined a cute puppy running around the loft until remembering Melanie is allergic), and a couple clothing boutiques with extravagant designs in their display windows. I take mental notes to come back and check them out.

Only a few people have walked passed me on the sidewalk and not one has hesitated to return a warm smile. One woman even complimented my black four-inch pumps. Hopefully she couldn't tell they are hurting my feet.

I will not make the generalization that everyone around here is a friendly citizen, but it did plant a homey feeling inside of me. Something strangers back home never seemed to do.

I swing open the doors of the apartment building and the cool air conditioning gives a welcome by blowing through my straightened hair. I love how the lobby always smells like a freshly prepared hotel room. And no matter who is maintaining the front desk, there is always a greeting extended as if we are long-time friends.

The elevator doors open and I take in my reflection as always. Fresh face with only lip gloss and mascara. A white blouse tucked into a gray pencil-skirt with a black blazer relaxing around my shoulders to tie the outfit together with my heels.

The perfect interview outfit.

I have worn this same outfit to all three interviews I have ever had in my life and it may be the reason why I always get hired.

The perfect, *lucky* interview outfit.

The elevator doors open to the fourth floor and I make my way down the hallway, pulling Melanie's access card out of my small black crossbody handbag. There are voices coming from inside as I swipe it across the reader. The green light blinks and I open the door.

"Hey, Tammy bear! How did it go?" Melanie acknowledges my entrance as she lies curled up on the couch in a yellow sweater and blue jeans. She has replaced the jet black bob haircut with long, black and wavy extensions. Her head is resting on Ronald's chest.

Ronald greets me with a smile and even in his casual wear, he remains dressed to impress. He is styled with a black v-neck t-shirt underneath a navy blue blazer with black jeans and navy blue boat shoes. A single gold chain is around his neck, sparking an urban flare into his attire.

"It went GREAT." I bounce down onto the part of the sectional sofa closest to the door. "I got the job! My orientation is next week!"

"Congrats!" Ronald says, "We'll have to take you to dinner to celebrate."

"Yes, I'm so happy for you," Melanie sits up. "Jobs are awesome. Orientations are so cool!"

I toss a pillow at her sarcasm and she laughs at her joke. "No, but really... That's great news. Do you like Japanese food? This is cause for some good hibachi." Melanie rubs her hands together and licks her lips.

"You guys don't have to take me anywhere. I'm just glad I have a legitimate way to contribute to you letting me stay here, Mel."

She blows a kiss at me and they persist to brainstorm potential dinner spots. My humility is ignored.

So I kick off my heels to throw my feet onto the couch and get comfortable, deciding to partake in the discussion. Any reason to indulge in fine dining and hibachi performances is nothing to fight against.

I can only imagine how often Ronald takes Melanie to luxurious restaurants that are decorated with romantic lighting and delightful entertainment. He probably buys a bottle of the finest champagne, then they eat their filet mignon that is placed strategically in the middle of their plates. Three pieces of asparagus and a small leaf placed beside it. The check resembling a car note or mortgage.

Give my compliments to the chef.

Staring at the couple, I keep wondering why Melanie insists they are not a couple. Why not just be together if this man has been here for you from the start? I understand she likes to point out the fact she never knew her father, but shouldn't that make her more inclined to hold on to a guy that treats her right and wants to be with her?

I guess it doesn't work that way.

My internal and external conversations are interrupted when Sabrina enters the apartment and slams the door behind her. The walls rattle and the sound echoes up into the high ceilings.

I turn around while Melanie and Ronald glance up, finding the Latina standing firmly with her arms crossed over her pink tank top. She has a look on her face that would rip Melanie's head off if it had the capability.

"Um... Hey, Bri?" Melanie says, squinting her eyes to read Sabrina's body language.

"I KNEW you were trouble the day I met you, Melanie."

Uh-oh.

My cousin stands from her seat. Ronald reaches for her but she pulls away. "What are you talking about?"

"You know EXACTLY what I'm talking about! One of your whore friends hooked up with MY man and YOU let it happen!" Sabrina's Spanish accent is emphasized through her raised voice that begins to shake in anger. She points her index finger maniacally at my cousin with every word that crashes against the air of the room.

Melanie scoffs and reclaims her seat next to Ronald, who is watching her as closely as myself, before answering her roommate. "Sabrina, maybe you should head into your room and collect yourself. We can revisit this topic when you've calmed down."

"No, bitch, I know all about your hoe ass and your hoe ass friends!" Ronald urges for Sabrina to watch her mouth. I remove my bag from over my shoulder.

There is banging at the door and Sabrina ignores it as she paces back and forth. "Running around town acting like you're role models. Claiming to empower women and be classy ladies. But behind closed doors you're dropping your panties for a few dollars."

Whoa.

My eyes widen at her words. Melanie jumps up from the couch with her fists balled jaw clenched. "You don't know anything about me, Sabrina."

"I know EVERYTHING about you! PUTA! If you want to sell your vagina to afford your half of the rent, that's your business. But once it involves Miguel it becomes my business too!" Sabrina digs into the brown purse on her arm. "You need some money, bitch? Here you go!" She throws a handful of twenty dollar bills into the living room at Melanie.

Red covers my cousin's vision as she dives at Sabrina only to be caught by Ronald before she can even reach the other side of the couch. "Babe! Calm down, calm down. She's not worth it..."

I stand up and try to comfort my cousin with him. The banging at the door continues and now Miguel's voice can be heard on the other side demanding to be let in.

Sabrina backs away and reaches into her endless purse again, pulling out a phone and waving it around. "Miguel's messages were filled with conversations about the deals your representatives make. The whole operation. The 'appointment' he had in the back of the club while you happened to be back there 'servicing' a client of your own! I know about everything!" Sabrina throws the phone like a fast-pitch at Melanie's head but misses. It cracks the glass of one of the windows before breaking into several pieces from the impact.

Before I could even think, I hop over the couch and grab Sabrina by her long brown ponytail. Tugging her body downwards I swing her into the breakfast bar and punch repeatedly. Ronald runs over to grab me, which unleashes Melanie. The chance of Sabrina making it out this apartment alive is lessened.

Realizing he could not break up the fight alone, Ronald opens the door. Miguel runs in and they work together to bring an end to the flying fists and hair grabbing that has toppled over the chairs of the breakfast bar.

Miguel carries a kicking and swinging Sabrina to the door. "I'm not spending another day in here with you! I'll send for my things and you better hope I don't send the cops too!"

Her face is red and nose is bleeding. The ponytail that was once slicked back to perfection is now a disheveled mess of hair all over her head.

Oops.

Ronald runs over to close the door upon their exit and prevents us from following them out into the hallway of the upscale complex.

My adrenaline rush decreases when he confirms that I'm okay. I notice the buttons of my blouse were ripped off in the scuffle.

Melanie is frozen leaning her body against the sofa table that is placed along the back of the couch. Her hands are on her head and she's taking deep breaths that are releasing like fire as she tries to come back down from the astronomical levels of rage that Sabrina has taken her to.

"Babe..." Ronald walks toward Melanie slowly. His hand is extended in hopes of bringing her into him before Mt. Melanie erupts.

But before he could reach her, Melanie picks up a thick vase full of fake decorative white roses from the table and heaves it through the window next to the one already damaged by Miguel's phone. Shards of glass shatter to the floor and out into the sky, sparkling under the sun as the flowers are released from the vase and gravity pulls them down and out of our sight.

"I am an escort. SHE is an escort group. But only for the wealthy and connected."

Melanie, Ronald, and I have taken our seats back on the couch. I stare at my toes, digging them into the plush carpet littered with twenty dollar bills. My ears are forced to endure Melanie's secret that is not so much of a secret anymore.

"It began as, purely what is seen from the outside… And slowly transitioned into a hybrid, where the second form of the business was only known by a select number of insiders."

"Did you know about it?" I look at Ronald who is watching Melanie as she finds comfort in picking with her nails.

"Sadly, I'm the one who brought her the idea. I was young and selfish."

Ronald goes on to explain how numerous men within or connected to the party industry had come to him with requests to take a representative of SHE to dinners or Christmas parties. They just wanted a beautiful woman on their arms to impress investors and colleagues. It was a market that was clearly willing to be financially gracious to the diverse women Melanie had gathered. Ronald saw the innocence in having them escort a man to a function in hopes that their beauty and elegance would make them look better to peers. When he pitched the idea to Melanie she thought of all the doors it may open. They could branch out from strictly club appearances and start making deals with these gentlemen to get her group into the professional public eye. So they gave it a chance and deals were sealed, allowing their participation in ribbon cuttings and motivational speeches. *SHE* was able to promote the importance and strength of women in our society on a greater scale. The group was expanding, the women were content, and their bank accounts were healthy. Ronald was able to finance his first venue from the cuts he earned in making the referrals. Life was grand.

Then sex came into play.

One of the representatives enjoyed herself a little too much at a yacht party she was attending for a client. After a number of drinks she allowed him to enjoy her a little too much as well in a cabin below the deck. The client was extremely generous in his tip that was transferred to Melanie's PayPal account, which prompted her to ask the girl how the evening went. She immediately admitted to what she did and was very apologetic, but the news sparked something within Melanie that was far from resentment: Intrigue.

So, the group slowly transitioned into a world of business that brought them loads of money they never thought would be seen. Melanie was brought into a life of luxury she had always deemed impossible to acquire and the rest of the ladies were there to enjoy it with her every step of the way.

But, Ronald began to regret the additions to the operation.

He cared about Melanie and it was not his intention to "pimp her" or plant the idea of high-end prostitution into her mind. When he asked her to stop, she refused. When he thought admitting his love for her would change her mind, it only made Melanie play on his guilt for getting her into it in the first place. She was ready to push him away, but he stayed by her side.

He stopped sending clients, but by then their client-base was growing on its own. So he made her promise that if she was going to keep doing this, she could only have appointments at his venues. This way they can be monitored by his security to make sure she was as safe as possible.

"When I was blowing up your phone looking for you and going through hell at *Illusion*, you were in the back of the club 'working'? Who was your 'client'?" My question shakes with anger and nervousness. As much as I want to understand their reasoning behind this entire ordeal, I was still having a hard time getting over the events of the other night. It was hard enough to do that while knowing nothing, and now that I know almost everything I am livid.

"The guy that came up to me at *the Crawlspace*. That was my client at *Illusion*." Melanie answers. A tear rolls down her cheek and she peeks up from her hands to look me in the face.

I recall what I saw that guy mouth to Melanie before leaving our section, '*One hour*', and I become even more upset. So, his "appointment" was in one hour. The clue was displayed right in front of my face.

Then there are the other times I can immediately remember where something someone said could have been a clue, but due to being unconcerned and uninformed there is no way I could have just read between the lines: Miguel talking about him and his friends coming out their pockets for Melanie's group, the creep at *Illusion* saying he wants to spend all his money on me, the guy in our section with the wad of money, and Jay betting he knew where my cousin was when she was M.I.A. Even his twisted assumption that I would let Dylan have sex with me is now understood.

All of this is exactly what Dylan was warning me about. This information is what he must have heard and knew about the *SHE* representatives.

This is why he wanted me to be careful.

All of those moments and words that could have delivered the truth if I wouldn't have blown them off. I was just too consumed with the freedom of simply being out here with the big cousin that I have always looked up to. The same big cousin who probably would not have confessed to anything if I displayed wariness. And even if I did hear the truth from Dylan or anyone else, I doubt I would have believed it. I would've continued to blow it off until I heard it from Melanie's mouth.

A lose-lose situation.

"So, this is why your girls drugged me. Because they are really a band of prostitutes, not the wholesome human beings they pretend to be," I laugh to keep from yelling. "All of this for an expensive car and name brand clothes, Mel? You brought this on yourself." The tears spilling out Melanie's eyes and Ronald's face of shame is making my blood boil. They are telling me they have been at this for years and suddenly, they want to feel sad and be repentant now that their big secret is revealed.

Screw that.

"It's not just about the expensive shit, Tamryn. You don't know what I've been through. You don't know what those girls have been through. Just because someone does what we have been doing, it doesn't make them any less human. It also doesn't give you the right to judge. We didn't all grow up the way you did. You still can't say they put something in your drink because you don't really know."

"Whatever. Okay, you didn't live the greatest life ever with Aunt Shannon and it was tough when Travis and TJ left but was it really bad enough to make you grow into a prostitute?"

Melanie jumps up from the couch. Ronald follows her sudden move to ensure she doesn't flip out again. "You have no clue how ignorant you sound right now. I am not justifying my actions but until you know what it feels like to be helpless and used, you'll never understand how critical it is to never be placed in that position again. Just leave it alone." Her tears have stopped and she is back to being angry in an attempt to defend herself.

I stand to combat her raised voice with own. "No, help me understand! I want to understand, Melanie! You tell me everything, what made you keep this secret from me for so long!? What did you go through that made you feel helpless? Never having Aunt Lucille around? Never knowing your dad? Who used you!?"

Melanie gets directly in my face. The few inches of height she has over me are making the air escaping her lips with every word brush against my forehead. "You wanna know all my secrets, Tam? TJ raped me. Yep. Years and years ago. Of course I never told you because why would I bring my innocent baby cousin into the dark place I was thrown into from my sanctity being ripped away? Just like I found no reason to tell you about all my endeavors out here. There are stems covered in thorns of pain from my past that continue to cut me deeply every single day, but guess what? I continue to blossom. I live my life to the best of my ability and refuse to play victim. I have learned from my mistakes and turned the biggest lesson of my life into strength. Fuel for my fire. Every time I hold a man down and assert my power, I replace the memory of my being held down and having my power taken away from me. And once you let your guard down for someone who claims to love you, you risk losing that power all over again. I remain in control at all times and treat trust as sacred as the virginity I was forced to lose. Now, I know this may have made me act a little crazy toward you and I am sorry. Dylan would probably never take your trust for granted, and I don't mean to try to build a wall around your heart the way I've done mine. I just can't help it. It seems like all my life I've been chasing after a love that I can believe in but I've, ultimately, made myself incapable of ever receiving it. It's like I'm trapped in my own freedom and the chance of having anything else taken away from me is too great a chance to take. I would never wish this on anyone..."

My chest hurts.

The irony of this situation is a hard pill to swallow, putting a lump in my throat and an aching in my stomach.

I blink and my own tears are released.

The only woman I have ever looked up to besides my loving mother. The only person in the world I could tell all my deepest, darkest secrets to and she was harboring one of her own. One that has been tearing her apart for years. She found solace in dealing with it through her paid sexual ventures, giving up on love, trust, and chances. Melanie placed herself in isolation with only her control and power to keep her warm at night. And she never allowed me the opportunity to save her the way she has always saved me, just to keep protecting my spirit.

Melanie is crying again now. She backs away from my personal space. "I know this is not what you came out here for. Looking at me right now must be like looking at a stranger. I can book you a flight back to Ohio. Maybe this isn't the right time for you to be here."

I wipe my face and step forward, grabbing Melanie's arms. "Are you kidding? This is the perfect time. All those years that you have been there for me, protected me, and made sure I was well... It's my turn to do that for you. You don't have to live like this, Mel. You can have your power without doing what you've been doing. And you can give a deserving man the chance to love you," I look to Ronald who is biting his lip nervously. "Everyone makes mistakes... This shit doesn't come with instructions. Sometimes we make the wrong things priorities and sometimes we let down our guard. It's all part of the process. It's all about taking chances. This move was a leap of faith for me. I came out here for myself, but now I have discovered that I have to stay for you. We will get passed this together."

Thirteen.

Cleveland, 2001

Melanie wouldn't say a word.

Without a willingness of her niece to provide an account of what occurred, Shannon was hellbent on having every male who was present in her house last night tested: Travis, TJ, and Joseph.

The rape kit could match the DNA of the attacker within the Federal Combined DNA Index System, but only if they had a record of prior arrests. She knew Travis had been in trouble with the law in his younger days, but what about the two young boys with no record?

They needed to be tested.

There was no fuss from Travis over cooperating. He took TJ out of school early to go to the hospital and was sure to speak with Joseph's parents.

While Melanie was being treated by nurses, refusing to speak, and having DNA collected from her body and clothing, the swabbing also commenced for the possible perpetrators.

It was of high priority that they contact Shannon with an answer as soon as possible, and she was given an estimation of three to four days. During this time, Travis and Shannon mutually agreed to pause their relationship.

There is a much greater possibility that Travis or TJ had something to do with what happened to Melanie. So Shannon could not bear to have either of them around, for the safety of her niece as well as herself.

It seemed as though once things were starting to really look upward, something so drastic and critical as this was destined to happen.

Shannon brought Melanie into her home to save her life in hopes that it would save Lucille's. She wanted Lucille to fall in love with the baby that she thought she did not want and therefore change her life for it. Even if it took a few months or years for Lucille to come around, she was eventually supposed to. The opportunity was always open. But, she never did.

So, Melanie became a permanent responsibility that Shannon was forced to live with. The only option she could have had would be to put her up for adoption, but

Shannon knew that would upset her own parents. So here she was, left with cleaning up yet another huge mess of Lucille's.

There was a permanent mop in Shannon's hand.

Every time Shannon looked at Melanie, she saw Lucille. Melanie, being a spitting image of her mother, was a constant reminder of Shannon's failure to help her sister. A reminder of the greatest defeat she ever encountered. As much as she did not want to see this when she looked at an innocent little girl, it persisted to cloud her vision year after year. The saddest part about it was she was pretty sure Melanie could tell.

When Mark passed away, it left her with a lonely heart. A new addition to the hurt within her life. He was her sole source of happiness and motivation, always spoke positively about Lucille and looked on the bright side of having Melanie. He kept Shannon's head held high even though they never wanted kids and having one in their household was taking a toll on their finances.

Shannon has never been one to question the Creator but she was left with no answers as to why such a critical person for her had to be taken away.

Until she ran into Travis Rene.

The gentleman with the beautiful soul who would do any and everything for her. The man who brought enough love into her life to make her forget about all the sorrow and pain. He made her heart feel whole again and overflown with an abundance of tenderness to begin raining onto Melanie. Tenderness and caring that she knew the young girl was yearning for.

Then this happened.

How would matters work themselves out after this? Her hands are tied in every possible scenario: If Joseph raped her niece, how did Travis allow it to occur? If TJ did it, he could never be around Melanie again. If it was Travis, she fell madly in love with a sick pedophile that was one hell of an actor.

There was no coming back from this.

The place Shannon had called home for most of her life had not been feeling too much like "home" ever since she and Melanie returned from the hospital. It is cold and filled with dark questions that were working to rip her apart all over again.

Shannon was sure to change the sheets on Melanie's bed once they arrived but, understandably, the preteen had not even gone up the stairs. Melanie had been utilizing the finished bathroom in the basement.

She took long baths prompting Shannon to knock on the door and hear Melanie's empty voice call out "Yes?" in confirmation that she was still breathing. These were one of the rare occasions where Shannon even hears her niece's voice. Melanie had been draped in agonizing silence since they have returned.

Worries such as these were the reasons why Shannon had not been going to work. She had to make sure Melanie was coping as well as she could. All she could do was pray she was near and dear when the young girl finally decided to open her mouth about what happened.

It was about 11:00 A.M. when Shannon was sitting on her chair in the living room. The television was on the *Food Network* and she was crocheting a scarf in preparation of Ohio's autumn months.

Melanie was curled up on the couch underneath a blanket. Her snores were faint below the sounds of chopping vegetables and instructions from the television. The landline telephone almost made Shannon's heart jump out her chest when the ringing blared like a fire alarm.

No one but her parents tend to call before noon and Shannon had not told anyone about what had occurred. So, she gathered herself and prepared her voice to have its normal tone in case she had to keep her parents unsuspecting. But she prayed that it's the hospital with the news she's been waiting for.

"Hello, this is Nurse Griffin from Hillcrest Hospital, is Shannon Williams available?"

Waiting time is up.

"I know you've grown to love TJ like a brother, but why didn't you tell me that he hurt you, Melanie?"

The blank stare pouring from Melanie's face was so desolate it's frightening. Shannon had been trying to make her niece speak ever since she hung up the phone.

Melanie maintained her silence as if there was no longer a soul occupying her body. She had become purely a vessel withdrawn deep within her thoughts.

Shannon got up from her chair and went into the kitchen to put on her shoes and a light jacket. She exited out the side door and into the driveway.

Melanie examined her hands and wrists.

She can still feel TJ's tight clench on them. Her eyes glanced in the direction of the side door shutting behind her aunt. Melanie knew she was the victim, but watching her Aunt Shannon she couldn't help but to feel empathy. All the things that she had gone through where Melanie's presence did not make matters any easier. All the problems where Melanie was a part of the issue at hand. Now this huge fiasco that would not have happened if she never chose to be selfish in the first place.

Then her embarrassing failure when she tried to fix it.

As much as Melanie wanted to believe in the fact that what TJ did was not her fault, she couldn't help but to feel accountable. It was her obsession with love and belonging that made her engage in the relationship with him, when all she needed to do was be patient and allow the nature of life to run its course. Because of Travis, Melanie would have had all the love and care she always wanted, but the look on her Aunt Shannon's face today had shown that this was no longer possible. Her life was ruined and she had caused yet another painful situation in the life of the woman who took her in.

There was no coming back from this.

With pessimism sinking into her mind and overpowering all other thoughts, Melanie contemplated running away. She sat on the couch and wondered why should she stay around when all she did was cause pain. Then she stared into the possibility of having a future similar to her mother's. One that had caused a great deal of sadness for the closest people to her by choosing to run away from her problems.

So Melanie redirected her focus. A new plan was constructed.

Once she turns eighteen, the world would be her oyster. She would travel and find a home for herself, because this place had made it clear that it was not meant to be that. She would not obsess over love, but instead find a way to fulfill her heart with power. No one would ever have the ability to hurt her, she would be free to do as she pleased, and she would remain in control at all times. She would never feel the way TJ made her feel again. But until then Melanie would be quiet and careful not to cause her Aunt Shannon anymore grief. Her Aunt Shannon whom was almost ready to love her until now.

"I won't press charges against him."

The cool wind from the late September weather blew against Shannon's face. She held her cellphone to her ear and listened to Travis' voice on the other line.

"Are you sure? I cannot believe he did this. I am pressed to take him to the authorities, myself. Actually, I will take him to the authorities."

His words brought tears to Shannon's eyes. The type of tears that formed when you knew something you loved and cherished must come to an end. "Don't do that, Travis. I just want all this to be over and I'm sure Melanie does too."

There was a brief silence on the other end of the phone until Travis' voice returned, filled with an amount of regret and shame that Shannon knew was killing him. "I know this is something we could never work through, Shannon... But, I really do wish this never happened. Not only for the well-being of Melanie, but because I truly do believe that you are my soulmate."

The first tears rushed down Shannon's cheeks. She wiped them away and walked further down the driveway, looking over her shoulder at the living room windows to be sure Melanie was not watching and trying to listen. This next bit of information that she must tell Travis could never fall into the knowledge of her niece. Shannon can only imagine the issues it may cause. "Travis, what was your last name before you changed it?"

There is another break of silence on the line. Travis gave the answer Shannon was afraid of. "Harper... Why, babe?"

Shannon's heart had officially broken all over again.

She closed her eyes and took a deep breath. Her voice remained strong as her body trembled from the oncoming sobs fighting to escape her body. "Travis, when they told me the DNA samples matched with TJ, they also told me something else."

"What? Wh-, Why did you want to know my last name? What else did they say?" Travis' tone raised an octave. A mixture of hope and confusion obliterated his mind. Maybe the news Shannon was preparing to reveal was something that would conquer this whole occurrence. A resolution that could keep them all together. Anything to make their love a possibility again. After being informed of what his son had done, there was nothing she could possibly say that could be any more surprising.

"You are Melanie's biological father."

Epilogue.

The sun is beginning to set.

I take in my surroundings as I lean against Melanie's Audi and wait.

The bright array of colors splash against the clear blue backdrop of the evening sky. The gentle breeze wafting through the slightly cool air, urging me to tuck my hands into the pockets of my long nude cardigan. The occasional car rolling by with its mysterious occupant.

When I wasn't learning the ins and outs of mocha lattes at the coffee shop, I was spending the weekend packing and cleaning with Melanie. Living out my suitcase had been a way of life for me ever since I arrived, so gathering my belongings was easy. All I had to do was borrow another suitcase from Melanie to accommodate the clothes and shoes I have purchased within the past few weeks and complete a few loads of laundry. But helping Melanie sort through her extensive collection of every clothing item under the sun is what took up most of the time.

Thank God Sabrina is the one who provided all the big furniture pieces in the apartment. And she had yet to collect her belongings as promised.

So, Melanie and I decided that she would pay her half to cover the last few months of the lease and we would get out of there. She even paid for the damages done to the two windows in the living room.

We also agreed that SHE Inc. would be remodeled into a brand new company. A different name and solid mission. No hidden attributes. The agreement officially put this apartment out of Melanie's price range.

Now the backseat of her luxury sports car is filled with bags. The small moving truck parked directly behind is crammed with Melanie's bedroom set (including the futon) and several more bags of her clothes and shoes.

I glance up as the side door of the building opens. Ronald steps out with bags of Melanie's clothes in his hands, followed by Melanie holding bags as well and Ronald's friend, Carter.

Carter is letting us rent the new empty guest house that is in the backyard of his home in the Hollywood Hills for a while.

"Alright that's all of it, Tam! Say goodbye to 'the 424'! I left the access cards in the mailbox like they told me to. It's time to get the hell out of here."

Ronald and Carter get in the truck while Melanie and I hop into her car. The smile spread across her face is contagious, filling my stomach with anxious and joyous butterflies.

In this moment I realize that my move was never strictly about myself. It was not the beginning of a new chapter where I run away from a life of contentment, with an attempt to find out who I am, and discover my dreams. It has actually always been the end of a completely distressing story. One that has been silently drawn on in the background for far too long.

It is a story about the little girl who has been trapped inside of Melanie, closed off and afraid of the past that haunts her. She has been hiding in plain view, closely overseeing that the grown woman she has become is doing everything she can to climb out the darkness she was cast into years ago. Melanie's judgment and actions have been manipulated by the fear of facing the event that she has buried deep inside with no intention of ever uncovering. Then the path of my life was utilized by fate to commence another important journey that has been long overdue: Giving Melanie the courage to extract her power onto coming face-to-face with what has happened. This is how she will set the little girl free and send her dark past away for good.

It is time to embrace a brighter future.

Made in the USA
Columbia, SC
02 May 2023

16048397R00157